In the Path of the Storm

The strength of the wind increased in power with every passing minute. In a patch of woodland, not too far distant, Badger urged his ancient limbs to greater efforts. He had travelled too far from his own set to be able to return in safety. He could think only of the alternative shelter where, unknown to him, his friends were already assembled. He was between the two and he knew he had put himself in the greatest peril.

By the same author:

The Ram of Sweetriver
The King of the Vagabonds
The Beach Dogs
Just Nuffin

The Farthing Wood Series:

Animals of Farthing Wood
In the Grip of Winter
Fox's Feud
Fox Cub Bold
The Siege of White Deer Park

In the Path of the Storm

Colin Dann

Illustrations by Trevor Newton

RED FOX

A Red Fox Book
Published by Random Century Children's Books
20 Vauxhall Bridge Road, London SW1V 2SA

A division of the Random Century Group
London Melbourne Sydney Auckland
Johannesburg and agencies throughout the world

First published by Hutchinson Children's Books 1989

Red Fox edition 1991

Text © Colin Dann 1989
Illustrations © Trevor Newton 1989

The right of Colin Dann and Trevor Newton to be
identified as the author and illustrator of this work
has been asserted by them in accordance with the
Copyright, Designs and Patents Act, 1988

Set in Baskerville by Speedset Ltd, Ellesmere Port

Printed and bound in Great Britain by
Cox & Wyman Ltd, Reading

ISBN 0 09 968890 5

Contents

In Memory of Frederick C. Brown,
friend and naturalist

Prologue

Whistler the heron stood in the shallows of the stream in White Deer Park one early morning in March. It was late winter. Or was it early spring? It was difficult to tell, as there isn't much difference between a mild winter and a cold spring. And the weather seemed to have stayed in the same pattern for months. There had been no snow; no ice. But there had been many gales and a great deal of rain. It was raining now. Whistler was supposed to be fishing, but the disturbance caused by the raindrops on the surface of the water made his prey harder to detect. He had fallen into a semi-doze, his slate-grey back hunched in its usual attitude. He was motionless.

From the fringe of woodland near the stream bank a towering figure emerged, his white coat ghostlike in the murk of the slanting rain. The Great Stag stepped sedately forward to drink. He noticed the heron but didn't disturb him. He was an old, wise animal who respected all other creatures in the Nature Reserve and he knew when to leave well alone. He knew Whistler was catching fish and he paused to drink with caution, making sure any ripples caused by his lowered muzzle didn't interfere with the bird's occupation. He drank and slowly raised his head.

Whistler came out of his reverie as he saw movement. He turned his head to the stag. As he looked the deer's body was seized by a sort of spasm and, quite suddenly, the legs collapsed and the great beast crashed on to his side. The stag seemed to tremble; then all was still except that, almost imperceptibly, the body began to slide down the muddy bank towards the stream where it became lodged, half in and half out of the water. Whistler launched himself into the air and, with a few flaps of his wings, reached the deer's side. The glassy look of the Great Stag's eyes and the beast's utter stillness confirmed the heron's fears. The leader of the White Deer Park herd was dead.

Whistler was so distressed he did not, at first, know what to do. The Great Stag had been so much a part of life in the Nature Reserve for the heron and for all his friends who had travelled there to seek sanctuary from their ruined birthplace, Farthing Wood, that he had epitomised the very name of their new home, White Deer Park. Not that it was such a new home to them now, for they would soon be entering their fourth season there. And now here was the lordly animal who had welcomed them into the Park on the first day of their arrival all that time ago, and whom all of them revered, lying lifeless at the heron's feet. It was just too much for Whistler to contemplate alone. He needed to share the burden. He took a last look at the sad sight of the great deer's carcass and flew hurriedly away.

His powerful wings took him quickly to that corner of the Park where his old friends had settled. The first creature he saw was Badger who was busy collecting fresh bedding for his set. Badger looked up as he heard the familiar whistle of the heron's damaged wing. The old animal's sight was very bad now but he knew Whistler so well by his sound that he didn't need to wait until he could see him properly. He called out a greeting in his gruff voice.

'Hallo, Whistler! More rain, more rain. Everything's sopping. My set's waterlogged and –' He broke off as the heron landed beside him and now even Badger could see the look of anguish in the great bird's eyes. 'Why, whatever's the matter, my friend?' he asked kindly. 'You look as if you've seen a ghost.'

'I – I have – almost,' Whistler stammered. He hadn't yet recovered from his shock. 'An awful thing, Badger. The Great Stag. . . .' His voice petered out.

'Well?' Badger prompted him.

'He – he's dead.'

'Dead?' cried Badger. 'Are you sure? I saw him only recently and –'

'He's dead, Badger,' Whistler repeated. His voice was hushed. 'I saw him die. Just a moment ago. It was horribly sudden. He was drinking at the stream and then – he – he just keeled over and lay still.'

Badger was stunned. He could scarcely believe it. 'How dreadful,' he murmured.

For a while neither spoke, lost in their own thoughts.

At last Whistler said, 'I suppose he was a great age.'

Badger said, 'Aren't we all, Whistler?' He was reminded of his own longevity. 'I don't know how I've survived when. . . .' He didn't finish. The rain still beat down relentlessly. 'I suppose I should get this bedding underground,' he mumbled.

'I'll tell the others,' Whistler informed him.

But Badger didn't hear. His thoughts were full of the momentousness of the heron's discovery. How would the Great Stag's death change things? Would the Park become a different place? He dragged the damp bracken and leaves he had gathered backwards into his set entrance. 'Never dry, never dry,' he muttered as he reached his sleeping-chamber. 'My old bones won't stand this for ever. I'm not immortal either.'

Later the rain ceased for a while. The animals from Farthing Wood, together with their friends and relations, had collected to bid farewell to the Great Stag as a mark of respect to an old acquaintance.

'It's the end of the old order,' said Fox. He looked about him. Vixen, his beloved partner, Weasel, Whistler, Tawny Owl and Badger met his eyes. They were all thinking the same thing. How long before they too would succumb? The stag's death seemed to bring their own a little closer.

'It's so sad,' said Vixen. There was a catch in her voice. 'He was a good friend to us all.'

'Who'll take his place?' Leveret asked. The young hare's question dispelled the older animals' gloomy thoughts. 'There will be a new leader, won't there?'

'There'll be a battle first,' Tawny Owl asserted. 'There's no obvious successor.'

'Someone will win through,' Weasel remarked. 'One of the younger stags.'

'Of *course* he'll be younger,' Tawny Owl said impatiently. 'That goes without saying, doesn't it?'

'I wonder who it'll be?' Mossy said anxiously. He didn't like change.

'We won't know that, Mole,' Badger said to him, 'until their breeding season. And that's a long way off.'

The body of the aged leader of the deer herd rocked gently in the rush of the swollen stream.

1

Owl is Discomfited

The weather continued very wet. Toad and Adder emerged from hibernation to see the Park wreathed in damp mists and the low-lying ground turned marshy. Toad was in his element. He loved such conditions and his warty skin glistened in harmony. But Adder grumbled. He craved warmth.

'We've come out too soon,' he moaned to his companion.

'Nonsense,' returned Toad, jumping up and down in his glee. 'Things couldn't be better.' Adder turned his back on him with a contemptuous hiss.

Toad leapt away to White Deer Pond and found it brimming over. The Edible Frogs were calling lustily to each other. One of them spied Toad and soon told him of the sad demise of the Great Stag. Like his friends from Farthing Wood, Toad was shocked. He remembered how the leader of the herd had befriended them all and Toad felt he wanted to be amongst his close companions now to share his sadness. He left the Pond without a word and travelled to the corner of the Reserve where he knew he would find his old friends. On the way he overtook Adder who was slithering through the mire with an expression of the utmost distaste on his face.

Toad broke the news to him. Adder halted. Never one to give vent to his emotions, the snake was nonetheless unable to prevent his expression wavering. And there was an unusually long pause before he replied simply, 'I see.' Toad knew Adder better than anyone and he guessed the news had had the same impact on the snake as on all the community. They continued their journey in silence.

They reached the area where their animal friends had settled, near the Hollow. It was a while before any of them put in an appearance. Tawny Owl was the first to see them from his perch in an oak tree where he was alternately dozing and watching. He flew down to greet them after their winter absence.

'Another season,' he remarked.

'Yes, and a sad start to it,' Toad replied.

Tawny Owl blinked sleepily. It was a while since the Great Stag had died. The deer carcass had been removed by the Warden and Owl had almost forgotten about it.

'He means the deceased beast,' Adder lisped.

Tawny Owl stared. Then, 'Ah! Yes,' he nodded. 'The Stag. It was by the stream, you know.'

Toad said with concern: 'There have been no other deaths? I mean –'

'No, no,' Owl cut in. 'None of us old 'uns. Badger's still around. And – well, so am I.'

'Evidently,' Adder drawled.

'And Fox?' prompted Toad.

'Oh yes. Fox and Vixen. And Weasel. And Whistler. It was Whistler who saw the Stag die.'

'He was a noble beast,' Toad said.

'Yes.' Even Adder concurred with that.

'There's another thing about the stream,' Tawny Owl resumed. 'There appears to be a dearth of food in it at present, according to Whistler. He has to go outside the Park to fish.'

The three creatures contemplated this but could come to no conclusions. Tawny Owl decided to return to his roost. He always slept a lot during the day.

'I'm going to find myself a dry spot – if there is such a thing,' Adder said. His red eyes glinted. 'But that won't do for you,' he addressed Toad. 'So I'll leave you to your own devices.'

'All right. I understand,' Toad answered. 'I'll stay around for a bit until I've seen some of the others. I'll give them your good wishes, shall I?'

'Do as you please,' Adder hissed under his breath as he slid away. He headed for Badger's set. '*That'll* be dry,' he told himself.

There were many births that spring amongst the Farthing Wood community and their descendants. The Farthing Wood Fox and his mate Vixen had lived to see their lineage reach the fourth generation. A grandson of Bold (their cub who had left the Park and not survived) was born whom Vixen swore was the image of his grandfather at that age. She and Fox watched his progress with great interest. He was named Plucky.

Spring turned into summer and everywhere there were rabbits, hedgehogs, squirrels, mice and voles who were White Deer Park animals through and through, but who owed their existence to their doughty fore-fathers who had travelled across countryside and Man's terrain to reach the Reserve. There were moles and weasels and hares. And toads, kestrels and herons. Soon there would be adders. Only Badger and Tawny Owl remained solitary. Badger was ancient now and didn't always know what he was about. He had become very forgetful. The younger animals loved and respected him.

But sometimes they teased Tawny Owl who had not yet entered real old age. Weasel, too, could not resist a gibe now and then.

'Well, Owl,' he said, 'when will you muster up the courage to go a-courting?'

'When I choose to,' replied the bird loftily.

'It seems to me you don't choose to,' Weasel continued. 'At least, not on the evidence of three seasons in the Park.'

'How would you know? Can you fly?' Tawny Owl retorted.

'I don't need to,' answered Weasel. 'Everyone knows you've never been seen in the company of a female.'

Tawny Owl didn't remain to hear any more insults. He flew away in a huff. But there was no relief for him. Pace and Rusty, two of the younger foxes now parents themselves, found his shelter and goaded him cheekily.

'Here's the only old bachelor left of the originals,' Pace remarked to his cousin.

'Poor old Owl – he can't find a mate,' Rusty added provocatively.

Tawny Owl tried to maintain his calm, moving to a higher perch.

'Have all the females been snapped up, Owl?' Pace persisted, raising his voice.

'Stop chaffing me,' Tawny Owl called down irritably. He was becoming ruffled. 'Haven't you got anything better to do?'

'Haven't you?' Rusty gibed.

'Perhaps not.'

'But think of all those lady owls dying for a word from you, the famous Owl from Farthing Wood,' Pace taunted him.

'They'll have to wait then, won't they?' Tawny Owl answered. He knew he was foolish to take any notice but their raillery was impossible to ignore.

'Wait for what?'

'For me to choose to visit them,' Owl said superciliously.

'Oh – oh. Hark at that, Rusty. Don't you think it might be *they* who haven't chosen Tawny Owl?'

'Must be,' agreed Rusty. 'After all, he *is* the only bachelor.'

'I'm NOT the only bachelor,' Tawny Owl screeched furiously. 'What about Badger?'

'Poor old Badger? He's almost senile,' declared Rusty. 'You can't count –' He broke off as he saw his mother, Charmer, approaching.

'What's going on?' she enquired. She sensed the young foxes were up to some mischief.

'They're baiting me,' Tawny Owl complained querulously.

'Why – whatever for?'

'It's only about his bachelorhood,' Pace explained.

'Whatever business is that of yours?' Charmer demanded angrily. 'Haven't you got responsibilities of your own now that are more important than being disrespectful to your elders? You leave Tawny Owl in peace. He deserves all the quiet he can get.' She lowered her voice. 'And why should you want to scoff at another's misfortune?'

The young foxes looked contrite. They hadn't really meant any harm. Unfortunately Tawny Owl had heard Charmer's last remark and was mortified. Misfortune? What did they take him for? He – Tawny Owl, one of the most revered inhabitants of the Reserve? *He'd* show them! He was seething. He flapped up from his perch so impulsively he almost banged his head on the branch above. But he extricated himself and, trying hard to recover his usual dignity, sailed away across the treetops. When he finally perched again he was a long way from where any of his unkind persecutors could get at him. His anger eventually subsided. But, though he could never have owned up to it, he had been well and truly hurt. And now he knew he had to do something to prove them wrong.

The trouble was, he knew most, if not all, of the female owls would already have paired off. However, he needed to find out for sure. So, in rather a half-hearted way, he began to make a tour of the Park and its nesting sites. He soon discovered that the other male owls were very jealous of their territory and would drive him off if he attempted to approach too close. It was a demoralizing experience for him. At night he concentrated on catching his prey and, while he ate, pondered on his next move.

'Nothing else for it,' he told himself. 'I'll have to extend my search outside the Park.' In a way he was quite relieved at this state of affairs. There would be a wider area to roam, with the likelihood of better opportunities of finding what he sought. And, best of all, none of his old companions – or new ones – would have any way of following his progress.

One night he flew out, over the downland, skimming effortlessly through the air on his silent wings. He looked back at the boundary fence of White Deer Park and the dark silhouettes of its trees. Although he often flew beyond the bounds of the Park, the significance of his flight this time made him feel just a mite apprehensive, since he didn't know for sure how long it might be before he would return there. But he turned his head resolutely and set a course for the nearest patch of woodland.

2

A Rendezvous

In May and June that season's White Deer Park fawns were born. The young deer were born with the usual dappled coats. It was only as they matured that the animals took on the white colouring that gave the Nature Reserve its name.

The Farthing Wood animals knew that amongst these newborns there was a future dominant male in whose veins the blood of the Great Stag was coursing. But the older creatures knew they would never know him. What they were interested in was which of the present mature stags would assume the role of the Great Stag's successor. At this time of the year the stags separated themselves from the hinds and wandered, sometimes together, sometimes alone. To the watching animals there already seemed to be one obvious contender for the leadership. He was the largest and sturdiest of the beasts and was certainly aware of his

strength. He was cool and self-possessed in the other
males' company and had a superior air. His antlers
were still growing but he already had a greater head
than his companions. He was known as Trey. The
animals were impressed by him and began to wonder
how they would fare in relationship to him.

'He's a proud creature,' Fox remarked when he and
Vixen stopped one evening to watch. 'Look at the way
he carries himself.'

'Yes,' Vixen agreed. 'He seems to realize even now
he has no real rivals. It's in his bearing.'

'There will be some challengers,' Fox answered her.
'It's in the nature of things.'

'My only concern is that he won't interfere with our
way of life or our friends',' Vixen said, voicing Fox's
own fears. 'It's been so peaceful since the departure of
the huge hunting Cat.'

'We'll keep ourselves to ourselves,' Fox vowed. 'No
creature can take exception to that.'

So the Farthing Wood community went about their
business as usual without upsetting anybody.

Badger had had a tenant for much of the spring in his
set, and an unlooked-for one at that. Because of the
long period of wet weather Adder had set up home in a
dry spot near the mouth of one of Badger's tunnels. He
had not asked permission and Badger was too old and
polite a friend to object. But when a drier patch of
weather set in and Adder showed no sign of wanting to
leave, Badger began to make some pointed comments.
It wasn't that Adder was there all the time. He couldn't
be. He had to go out to catch his food. Yet the way he
used the set as his base, constantly returning to it as if

he had some kind of right, really got under Badger's hide.

One bright morning when the snake didn't seem at all disposed to stir Badger said: 'Why don't you go for a sunbathe? I thought you didn't like temperatures too cool?'

Adder grinned enigmatically. 'There's quite enough warmth to suit me here, thank you, Badger,' he replied.

'Isn't it time you ate?' Badger hinted. 'I don't think you've moved for days.'

'I don't need to hunt every day,' was the reply and Adder coiled himself up even more comfortably. 'I suppose you couldn't spare a few more of those dry leaves for this corner?' His tongue flickered in and out as he savoured the smell of the bedding.

'No, I couldn't,' Badger said shortly. 'I'm not your housekeeper. I didn't mind sheltering you during the constant downpours. I like company. But there are times when I also like solitude.'

Adder ignored him. He merely stared straight back at Badger with a blissful expression on his face. Badger lumbered away, growling to himself.

Later Mossy visited his ancient friend via one of the mole's connecting tunnels that led straight into the set. Badger immediately began talking about Adder as if Mossy had been there all day. 'He's taken up permanent residence here,' he complained. 'Snakes should find their own burrows. What am I to do, Mole?'

Mossy didn't consider he was in a position to advise. 'You've known Adder much longer than I,' he replied. 'I wouldn't dream of –'

'And then, what do you think?' Badger continued

without listening. 'He wants his bedding provided. He always had the cheek of all his kind but this time – well!' He lapsed into peevish mutterings.

Mossy thought it best to change the subject. 'Have you seen Tawny Owl recently?' he enquired.

'What? What? Owl? No, I haven't. What of it?' Badger answered irritably.

'I met Weasel earlier. He says he thinks Owl's disappeared. No-one's seen him since – um – well, since. . . .'

'Since what?' Badger snapped.

'Since the young foxes badgered him,' Mossy finished and tittered nervously.

'Very amusing, Mole,' Badger commented humourlessly. But he was interested. "What's this all about?' he asked.

Mossy explained. 'Weasel told me the tale. He was involved too. He admitted it. They've been goading Tawny Owl because of his solitariness.'

'Nothing wrong with solitariness,' Badger replied at once. '*I'd* relish it.'

'That wasn't quite what I meant.' Mossy went on to describe the circumstances.

'Oh,' said Badger. 'I see. Poor old Owl. Why treat him like that? And he's disappeared, you say? Disappeared where? To another quarter of the Park?'

'Weasel says not. It seems Whistler hasn't seen Owl flying over any part of the Park for ages.'

'Well, we can't let this rest. Perhaps he's keeping to his roost. He could be ill.'

'None of his favourite haunts are occupied. Whistler's been to look. Weasel is convinced Owl's left the Park.'

Badger was really concerned. 'Oh no. That would be awful. Driven out like that! I hope the young foxes have been –'

'They're very upset about it,' Mossy interrupted. 'Weasel told me.'

Adder had heard the voices coming from Badger's far chamber. He put two and two together. 'The bird's gone searching for a mate,' he hissed under his breath. 'How absurd at his age.'

Badger trundled up the tunnel to give Adder the news.

'I heard,' Adder said abruptly. 'Well, Badger, I think we can look forward to a long absence from our friend Tawny Owl.'

'How can you be so unfeeling?' Badger demanded.

'Not unfeeling; just realistic,' Adder answered, quite unperturbed. 'Old Owl's not exactly a glossy-plumed youngster, just out of the nest.'

'I shall speak to Fox,' Badger said determinedly. 'We must do something. Bring Owl back.' He lumbered away.

'And how do you propose to do that? Sprout wings?' Adder called after him sarcastically.

Mossy followed faithfully in Badger's footsteps for a while. Adder watched them go. 'I suppose they'll mount a search,' he muttered. But the topic of Tawny Owl had reminded him of a search he had been contemplating making himself now that there was dry summer weather. He had expected – perhaps had even hoped – to come across Sinuous in his wanderings. But he hadn't done so. Adder had a feeling, though, that he knew one place where he could find her. It was a favourite spot of the she-viper's, near the stream. So, despite his comfortable surroundings, he issued forth from the set into the sunshine.

Since the death of the Great Stag the stream had generally been avoided by the Farthing Wood animals. Without actually giving voice to their feelings, the stream had become for them a place of portent. That the stag had died on its banks was like an omen. It gave the site an air of mystery. Whistler was unable to fish there. And the long wet spell had made it unnecessary for use as a drinking place. However, all this was immaterial to Adder as he slithered over the ground, bent on his rendezvous.

Sinuous detected his approach before he saw her. She was sunning herself on a mossy patch amongst the new young ferns. She lay on slightly rising ground. She observed Adder a few metres distant, his tongue darting incessantly as he sought for her scent. Sinuous allowed her face to take on the typical grin of the snake; a sort of leer. She was pleased and a little flattered Adder had come looking for her.

When Adder was close by, she said: 'Our trails cross at last. I've been wondering why it hasn't happened before?'

Adder slid to an abrupt halt at the sound. He didn't wish it to be too obvious that he was on a search. He looked up and saw Sinuous on her couch of moss. 'I haven't been in these parts for a while,' he told her.

'I'm well aware of that,' Sinuous answered. 'What brings you here now?'

'Oh well, one has to go somewhere,' Adder said dismissively.

The she-adder's grin broadened. Her tongue picked up Adder's scent. 'Have you been travelling in a hurry?' she asked archly.

'Um – well, not particularly,' Adder fibbed. 'But my movements are always more lively on a warm, sunny day.' He moved closer. 'The wet weather kept me rather under wraps, as it were,' he joked.

'And in all that time, didn't you spare a thought for me, Adder-of-the-blunt-tail?'

The snake pondered his reply. He *had* thought about her, though only intermittently. 'Oh yes,' he said. 'I think about everyone and everything from time to time.'

'Non-committal as ever,' Sinuous summarized. Her tone changed. 'It's been so quiet here. Almost lonely. Ever since the stream. . . .' She did not complete the sentence.

'Since the stream what?' Adder prompted.

'Became out of bounds.'

Adder considered. 'You were going to say something else at first, I think?'

'No – o,' Sinuous said slowly. 'No, not really. Only that it's as though the animals have become afraid of it.'

'Because of the Stag's death?'

'There may be more to it,' she suggested.

Adder held her gaze. Was she giving him a warning? 'I don't plan to swim there,' he informed her.

'No. Nor I. But there are creatures who are more partial to watery pursuits than we snakes. Toads, for instance . . .'

3

Familiar Terrain

By the time Badger was discussing the bird's where-
abouts with Fox and Vixen, Tawny Owl was far away.
He had met with no luck in any nearby woods or copses
and so had flown on further. Prey was easy to find and
so were places to roost during the daylight hours. But
his quest for a partner proved elusive.

It wasn't long before certain features of the landscape began to strike chords in Tawny Owl's memory.
This was because he had travelled over it before, from
the opposite direction, on the epic journey to the
Nature Reserve – oh! so long ago. He began to recall
events that had occurred at certain places which he
now recognized, or what had been said by one of his
friends at a particular spot. It was uncanny. Many of
those friends he remembered were now gone. Yet they
seemed to live on in this countryside. He perched in an
oak and looked up at the gleaming sky. He seemed to

see Kestrel, hovering, keen-eyed, a speck in the blue, spying out the land ahead. What a flier he had been! An aerial acrobat.

Tawny Owl shook the memories away. He must concentrate on the present and on his new purpose. He rested and as he dozed he dreamed. He dreamed of his old home and his birthplace in Farthing Wood. And at dusk he awoke with a jolt and with a new idea. Why shouldn't he fly back there? Retrace the animals' historic journey? Back to their beginnings, to the place of their forefathers. Of course it would be changed, massively changed. He knew that. But whatever was left, whatever was there now, still enshrined the old home they had all shared all those seasons ago. And perhaps there was still a corner with a few trees where he could stay awhile and survey the new landscape. What a story he would have to tell on his return to White Deer Park! And somewhere on his journey, over all that wide expanse, he would be bound to find that special companion to fly with him. . . .

The more he thought, the more excited Tawny Owl became. He felt younger in spirit than he would ever have dreamed possible again. But he needed to be cautious. For he wasn't young. He must fly within his capabilities; not take risks nor indulge in any foolishness. There was plenty of time. He was very pleased with himself and he flew a little loop around the oak tree to celebrate. His stomach, however, soon reminded him of the necessity of keeping his strength up and he set himself without further ado to obey its commands.

His hunting techniques were born of long experience. He knew where to look and listen for shrews and wood mice. Soon he had caught and eaten enough to sustain himself. Then he flew well above the tree tops towards a much higher landmark that loomed on the horizon, a shape blacker than the dark sky that surrounded it. Tawny Owl had recognized it and now flew unerringly towards it. It was a church tower.

Flying high as he was he naturally headed straight for the open belfry. He landed on a stone sill and glanced around. 'I've been here before,' he murmured. It all seemed so familiar. This church had been the Farthing Wood party's last sheltering place before reaching White Deer Park. Owl's head swivelled round and he looked out at the sky. The stars glittered.

'I'll shelter here again,' he decided. 'It's an ideal spot. No-one to disturb me here.'

He watched the night sky pensively, his thoughts turning once again to those long-ago events inside the church during the animals' previous visit. Presently dawn glimmered in the east. Tawny Owl's head drooped. He shifted his talons, then closed his eyes. He was soon asleep.

But he wasn't allowed to sleep for long. Because there were other occupants of the church belfry who, in the gathering dawn, began to return there from their nocturnal hunting flights. And they objected to the presence of a large bird at their roost.

Tawny Owl half awoke as something zipped past his ear. He opened one eye but saw nothing. Then the little snap! of noise came again. Now he was quite awake. He was curious. He opened both eyes fully and looked around. Against the pale backdrop of the lightening sky he saw a number of small darting creatures criss-crossing on their different swooping flights. Occasionally one would dart directly at the church tower, then veer away at the last second. More and more swelled these numbers. Some came close enough to Tawny Owl to glance at him but none of them dared do more than chatter at the intruder, before they flitted away again. The big bird of prey unsettled them. They were angry, but wary of him. Tawny Owl realized he had usurped the resting place of a colony of bats.

The tiny animals fascinated yet irritated him. He admired, as only a bird could, their flying dexterity. But he wanted to sleep and the bats made this impossible. Evidently they wished to sleep, too, during the coming daylight, yet none of them was sufficiently bold to enter the belfry. They chivvied and chided him, but Tawny Owl refused to be dislodged. They buzzed around and past him in a miniature aerial bombardment.

'Will you stop this annoyance?' he cried at them. 'I'm staying put.'

The bats paid no heed but continued their dive-bombing.

'I just want to sleep,' Tawny Owl hooted. 'Can't you leave me alone? You'll get no rest either!'

'Fly away, begone.' 'Move away, leave our roost.' The bats shrieked at him in their tiny high-pitched voices.

Tawny Owl lost his temper. He launched himself from the stonework and swooped into their midst, scattering the animals briefly before they resumed their skimming, skipping flights all around him. Wherever he flew they followed him. But he could never catch any. They could turn and bank in a fraction of a second and reappear a moment later in a different spot. All around the sky the bats darted in varying patterns and directions, never colliding and never settling.

Aggravated as he was, Tawny Owl watched their effortless skill with wonder. He felt himself to be clumsy and cumbersome by comparison. He didn't relish being outshone in the field of flying. Disgruntled, he returned to his perch on the stone sill. The bats resumed their skirmishes. Tawny Owl moved further inside the belfry and perched on a rafter. He put his head under his wing and tried to ignore the animals' squeals and squeaks. It was in vain. His patience was now entirely exhausted.

'How dare you keep this up!' he thundered. 'Do you know who I am? Tawny Owl from Farthing Wood!' He waited for the expected result of this piece of information.

The bats, however, had either never heard of him or treated the news with disdain. Their behaviour changed not at all.

'This is intolerable,' Tawny Owl moaned to himself. 'First I'm driven away from the Park by insults and goading. Now I'm starved of sleep by puny little creatures no bigger than a vole. What have I done to deserve this? I won't be driven out!' he declared finally. 'I want to rest!' he screeched. 'I don't want to eat you. I want nothing to do with you! If I can ignore you, can't you all just do likewise?'

For a brief period the bats stayed outside the belfry, their movements less frantic and antagonistic. They seemed to be communing with one another. Then, chattering and muttering together, they flew into the belfry and began to hang themselves upside down, one by one, from their favoured roosting spots. Their little long-eared heads turned all in one direction as they gazed at Tawny Owl.

At last one piped up: 'How do we know you won't eat us while we sleep?'

Tawny Owl fixed the tiny furry creature with his enormous eyes. He realized the bat's face was up the wrong way so he tried to accommodate him by twisting his own head as far as he could in order to meet his eyes. In doing so he very nearly toppled from his perch. The sudden movement startled the bats and they began to leave their places and dart about again.

Tawny Owl was beside himself. 'Stop it! Stop it!' he begged. 'Calm yourselves, please. I can't hang upside down like you so we'll just have to talk to each other the – er – wrong way up, if you see what I mean.' He waited until they were more or less settled again. 'Look,' he said, 'I don't eat bats. I couldn't catch you if I wanted to. And as for eating you while you're asleep, how could I do that if I'm asleep myself?'

He looked around at the little bodies, each of which seemed to be swaying gently from one leg. 'I've already eaten,' he rejoined to doubly reassure them. 'I'm not hungry. Only weary. I sleep through the daylight hours just like you. When it's dusk I'll depart. Is that a bargain?'

There was a barrage of squeaky voices. Then one rose above all the others. 'We won't bargain with you,' the bat said, 'because we can't trust you. We don't know who you are. So one of us will stay awake all day in case you mean to take advantage. That's our answer.'

'You're silly little creatures, all of you,' Tawny Owl said derogatorily. 'I always keep my word. Haven't you ever heard of the Oath of the Animals of Farthing Wood?'

There was silence. Owl took this as assent. 'Well, the Oath can be extended to any other animals we choose,' he informed them grandiosely. 'So if I extend the Oath of Mutual Protection to you, your safety is assured, isn't it?'

None of the bats chose to respond. Most of them hadn't the faintest idea what the bird was talking about. Some of the older animals did have an inkling of the legendary Oath that Owl was referring to, though they didn't understand enough to realize how it could be applied to the bat community. So silence reigned as they tried to puzzle it all out.

Silence was the one thing that Tawny Owl craved. In a trice he had fallen asleep while the diminutive animals kept themselves awake by their perplexity.

The sun rose steadily in the sky. Tawny Owl slept. Many of the bats still fidgeted. The sun reached its zenith. Tawny Owl slept on peacefully. Some bats shifted their skinny wings as they watched him. The sun slipped slowly down to the horizon. In the afterglow Owl awoke refreshed, stretched his wings and awaited dusk. When it was quite dark he prepared to fly on. All around the belfry tower the suspended bats were fast asleep. Tawny Owl left the church behind with a chuckle.

The lights of a nearby town drew him onwards. He flew well above its buildings and when he had crossed it he looked for another landmark to guide him. The distant but steady hum of heavy traffic reminded him of his direction. He flew over some farmland and alighted in a tall ash whose late-opened leaves were still a fresh new green. From here he could see the dazzling lights of the motorway traffic streaking across the foreground like miniature shooting stars. But the terrifying dangers of such a man-made obstacle as this great highway were no barrier to a bird. Tawny Owl looked on almost scornfully. All at once his reverie was interrupted. An owl had hooted from another tree. Or was he mistaken? He strained his ears to catch a repetition above the roar of the machines. Sure enough the call was repeated.

Tawny Owl replied with the answering call. 'Kee-wick.'

The stranger owl's next call was nearer at hand. Tawny Owl located it amongst a stand of poplars planted as a windbreak at the border of a field. He was confident the calling bird was a female and that she had noticed him and wanted him to come closer. So he obliged.

He alighted on the neighbouring tree to where the other owl was perched.

'I've been watching you,' said the bird who was indeed a female.

'Watching me?'

'Yes, for quite a while. I saw you roosting at the church building and your battle with the bats.'

'Battle!' Tawny Owl exclaimed contemptuously. 'There was no battle. Only a minor irritation.'

'Your flight is very purposeful,' was the next observation.

Tawny Owl took this as a compliment. 'I'm on a journey,' he explained.

'A journey? To where?'

'To an old territory of mine.'

'What for?' the female owl enquired. She sounded intrigued.

'Oh, it's a long story,' Tawny Owl replied. 'I'm flying to an old hunting ground I used to frequent.'

'Is the hunting good?'

'I don't know any more. It used to be when I lived there. But there have been changes.'

'Then why go back there? Can't you find what you want round here?'

Tawny Owl was struck by the aptness of her question, innocent though it was. 'That depends,' he answered with a sideways look at her that was intended to be full of meaning.

The female owl didn't notice the significance of his expression. 'Depends on what?' she fluted.

'Well – you know.' Owl ruffled his wings impatiently. 'Certain things. How much of the terrain is occupied and – er – by whom. . . .'

'What difference does that make? Can't you defend yourself?'

'Of course I can!' he answered huffily. 'I meant, is the area fully marked out and – er – claimed?'

The female owl looked at him for a long time before

answering. 'Now I see why you're returning to your old area,' she surmised. 'You haven't paired.'

This was a sore point with Tawny Owl. He shifted his stance and the slender poplar branch rippled elastically. 'No, no, I haven't paired,' he admitted grumpily.

'Small chance round here for you then,' the female informed him. 'You'd better press on.'

Tawny Owl glared. 'But you – you were calling. Where is your mate then?'

'Collecting food, I hope,' she answered. 'He's been gone a long time. My babies are almost fully fledged. They're always hungry. They never stop nagging for food so I've been trying to hasten his return. They've eaten all we've brought them.'

The last thing Tawny Owl wanted to hear about was the details of other owls' family life, especially in his present predicament. He hastened to be gone.

'I must be on my way,' he muttered and leapt from his branch.

'Where do you head now?' she called after him.

'Farthing Wood,' he hooted, 'if it's still there.' He tarried no longer but sped straight for the motorway. The female owl watched with beak agape. Abruptly she concluded just whom she had been addressing. The Farthing Wood Owl!

4

Trey

Badger's concern about his old friend Tawny Owl's disappearance was shared by Fox and Vixen.

'To think of one of the elders of the Farthing Wood community feeling himself forced to quit the Park!' Fox bemoaned. 'It's outrageous and Pace and Rusty must be reprimanded. They may think they're grown-up foxes but their behaviour shows otherwise. I shan't take them to task myself. Their own parents have that duty to perform.'

'But in the meantime, Fox, what can we do to get Owl back?' Badger wailed. 'I think he's too old to go off scouring the countryside on some fool's errand such as this.'

'Don't worry, my dear friend,' Fox answered. 'We'll think of something.'

'Does Owl actually plan to stay outside the Reserve?' Vixen queried.

'As far as I can tell he intends not to return until he has someone to accompany him,' Badger replied. 'I think Weasel could tell you more about how all this arose.'

'Weasel? Yes,' Fox mused. 'He and Owl always had their differences, didn't they? Seemed to have a penchant for needling each other unnecessarily. But Weasel ought to know better than to joke about vital things like pairing off. You say he's partly to blame, Badger?'

'Yes, I'm sure of it. He couldn't have foreseen the result, of course,' he added, trying as ever to smooth things over.

'I think we should have a word with Weasel,' Fox asserted. 'The onus is on him to help in this matter. Come on; he's bound to be around close by.'

There was no difficulty in finding Weasel but he didn't prove to be very disposed to help.

'What can I do?' he asked them coolly. 'Tawny Owl's simply gone off in a huff. He'll be back soon enough when he's recovered himself.'

'Really, Weasel, I don't know what you were thinking of, talking to him the way you did. You know how touchy he is,' said Fox.

'I wasn't to know he would go to such lengths,' was Weasel's answer. 'Do you think I'd have said a word if I'd known he'd be so nonsensical?'

'You always have enjoyed teasing him,' Fox recalled.

'Yes, but . . . well, he's never reacted so extremely before, has he? It's no use worrying yourself, Fox. Nor you, Badger. We're past the age when we could mount missions of rescue.'

Fox looked at Weasel's grizzled fur with a wry expression. 'Yes,' he said. 'Our colouring complements each other.' He was only too aware of his own greying coat. As for Badger, he hadn't even regained his breath.

'But we can't desert Tawny Owl, can we?' Vixen pleaded.

'We haven't done so, Vixen,' declared Weasel. 'He's deserted *us*, hasn't he? Purely in a fit of pique. There's just nothing to be done – except wait. Even if we were still our young adventurous selves it would be quite impracticable for mammals to go searching for a bird.'

'Oh dear, he could be far away by now,' Badger wailed. 'And I don't think he's any better equipped than we are to deal with the perils outside the Park.'

'Of course he is,' Weasel said kindly, trying to comfort. 'He has wings to carry him above any danger. Now don't fret. I'm certain we shall soon see –' Weasel stopped suddenly. He was looking away over their heads at something in the background. The others followed his glance.

It was Trey the large white stag that Weasel was looking at. And Trey was looking at them. He was on his own. He stood stock still and stared haughtily. Then, with a proud toss of his head, he began to step sedately towards them. He was a fine powerful-looking beast.

'You're some of the old travellers who came here long ago from another place, if I'm not mistaken,' he said without preamble. He had a harsh voice.

'Yes,' said Fox. 'We are.'

'You realize, I suppose, we only tolerate your presence here, we don't invite it?'

'Tolerate? Presence? What are you talking about?' demanded Fox. 'And who's "we"?'

'The herd, naturally.'

'Oh, you've been elected to speak for all of them, have you?' Weasel interjected sardonically.

The stag gave the tiny animal a contemptuous look as if such a midget wasn't even worthy of an answer. 'I am now the natural leader of the herd,' he said, addressing the two foxes and Badger, 'and therefore I wish you to understand your position.'

Fox ignored the last remark. 'I should have thought some of the other stags might have something to say about whether you're the natural leader?' he suggested. 'That's if I have learnt anything about the pattern of a deer herd's behaviour during my time in the Park.'

'Who is there to challenge *me, Trey*?' he asked boastfully. 'I am a royal stag. Have you ever seen antlers as splendid as these?'

'Yes,' Vixen replied coolly. 'The Great Stag, your precursor, had finer ones in his heyday.'

Trey glowered. But he was honest enough to admit, 'He was a superb specimen, it's true. But,' he added, 'his heyday was over long before he died. Now he's gone things will change – and not just in the herd.'

'We'd like to know about these changes,' Badger spoke for all of his friends, 'since we live here too.'

'Exactly,' Trey said. 'You live here too. We deer have allowed all you smaller animals to do just that, whereas in reality this Nature Reserve was set aside for us alone. We gave the Reserve its name. The Park belongs to us. Do you think for one moment, if it hadn't been for such a rare and valuable white deer herd, that this area of land would have been reserved for paltry common or garden creatures such as yourselves?'

The animals were open-mouthed.

'You don't answer me,' prompted Trey.

'We are dumbfounded by your arrogance,' Fox answered the stag. He drew himself up. 'I'm old now,' he said. 'But I also have authority and am respected in this Park. Your ancestor would never have spoken to me – or any of us – like that. I'd like to see you brought down to earth. You'll have rivals, sure enough, in due season. Then perhaps you'll find brute strength is more than a match for conceit.'

'The only thing I shall find,' said Trey, 'is every foolhardy rival running from my lowered antlers, one by one. And I mean to be not only the leader of the deer herd but Lord of the Reserve. So you must stay in your corner of the Park, all of you. I want no interference with my herd's grazing. The most succulent shoots, the sweetest grasses, the tenderest leaves are ours alone. Smaller creatures must make do with our leavings. Otherwise you'll be permitted here no longer. So tell your friends the rabbits and hares and suchlike to keep clear. You've all had the run of our Reserve for too long. And what have you brought us in return? Nothing but mayhem: a succession of dangers in what was once a place of tranquillity. You Farthing Wood animals are our Bad Luck.' With that he turned on his heel and walked away with a distinct swagger.

The friends were speechless. They could find no answer to Trey's accusation. At last Vixen murmured, somewhat defensively, 'I'm sure the rest of the herd don't see us that way.'

'Of course they don't!' Weasel exclaimed vehemently. ' "Bad Luck" indeed.'

Fox said: 'We're going to have trouble with that animal. I know it. "Lord of the Reserve",' he quoted. 'A rather premature claim, I feel, but it gives us all an indication of his intentions. I don't know what he meant about dangers and mayhem, do you?' He appealed to his companions.

Badger surprised them. 'I have an inkling,' he admitted. 'It's something that's been in my mind from time to time.'

'What, trouble that we've brought to the Park?' Weasel demanded angrily.

'No, no, Weasel, of course not,' Badger pacified him. 'It'd be more true to say that trouble seems to have followed us.'

Fox looked serious. 'Go on, old friend,' he urged. 'Let's hear your thoughts.'

'Well, I've often considered the irony of our lives here,' Badger resumed. 'Maybe you have too. After all, we journeyed here over hostile terrain, at great risk to ourselves the whole way, believing we were coming to a safe haven in the Nature Reserve. All along, during that arduous journey, it was that thought that buoyed us up. Yet it's been far from a safe haven. The first winter after we arrived we nearly starved to death. Then there were the poachers shooting at all and sundry, but particularly the deer. So Trey was right about *that* danger. Somehow we struggled through that winter to find ourselves the following spring involved in a war with other inhabitants of the Park led by Scarface. To cap it all, last summer a huge hunting animal prowls the Park, picking off its victims at will without any of us being able to mount any resistance to it. If we'd wanted a life of constant adventure and hardship we couldn't have chosen a better site! Quite honestly, I sometimes wonder if it wasn't more peaceful in Farthing Wood.'

'There's a lot of truth in what you say,' Fox avowed. 'The important thing though, surely, is that we've survived all of it. And the reason for that is that we've pulled together; helped one another. It wasn't like that in Farthing Wood. We were all following our own paths. The Farthing Wood animals were brought together by our journey in a unique way. We had one common aim. And that spirit has continued ever since. For that alone we should rejoice we came to White Deer Park. And I think some of our beliefs have been passed on to our descendants. The dangers that have occurred here would have occurred anywhere else. There's no such thing as a sanctuary entirely free of danger for wild creatures. Not anywhere.'

'The stag Trey seems to think otherwise,' Weasel observed.

'He's blaming us for a set of coincidences,' Fox answered. 'We weren't responsible for inviting danger here. The poaching men with their guns came because this is a Deer Park, not because the animals of Farthing Wood chose to take up residence here.'

'The thing is: what do we do about his threat?' Weasel asked. '*I* don't intend to be intimidated. I'll go on roaming the whole area of the Reserve. Why should we be holed up here? It'd be like the Great Cat's thraldom all over again.'

'It won't make any difference to me,' Badger said. 'I hardly venture further from my set than the nearest meal. Unless I need to see you dear friends. But even that I find taxing these days. My sight's so bad. . . .'

'Yes, we know,' Weasel cut in before Badger developed the theme. 'But I really don't think the threat was aimed at an old creature such as yourself.'

'We'll continue to live our lives as we choose to,' Fox said resolutely. 'Trey's a powerful beast and could be a formidable adversary. But his words may all be bluster. His apparent dominance of the herd may have gone to his head.'

'What of the smaller animals?' Vixen prompted. 'He mentioned the rabbits and hares.'

'We'll warn Leveret to be cautious and to spread the word,' Fox answered. 'But we'll call Trey's bluff.'

'We've been diverted, haven't we?' Vixen reminded them. 'We never did decide what to do about Tawny Owl.'

'Yes, we did,' Weasel contradicted. 'Wait for him to return. *That's* what we'll do. I bet he'd love to think he's put us all in a pet by his absence.'

'Perhaps Whistler will sight him somewhere,' Fox said. 'He's such a silly old owl sometimes.' He sighed. 'But Friendly *must* reprimand the youngsters. They look up to him.'

There was nothing more to discuss and the friends parted.

Over on the other side of the Park, Leveret, the young hare, was munching the juiciest stalks he could find, oblivious of the altercation with Trey. Every so often he raised himself on his hind legs amongst the tall grasses to scan his surroundings. His prominent eyes and sensitive ears were invaluable in detecting the slightest hint of an alarm. His speed, like that of his father, the Farthing Wood Hare, was legendary. Nothing in the Park could catch him, not even the deer. Not that they tried to do so. Prior to the old White Stag's death, the deer herd had lived equably with its neighbours. And it might have been because of this that Leveret was not quite so alert all of the time as he would have been outside the Reserve.

The grasses and vegetation, generally, were particularly lush that year in the Park, thanks to the long rainy spell. So there was more than enough for everyone. The insect population thrived and there was a glut of caterpillars and grubs. The birds found food easily for their nestlings and the Park's inhabitants enjoyed a period of plenty. Trey, however, was not content with this. He wanted to be acknowledged by all as the paramount being of the Reserve's animal kingdom. He therefore lost no opportunity to enforce this idea. Whenever he could make his presence felt he did so in some way, sometimes bullying, sometimes threatening. The animals resented this but there was nothing they could do about it except long for the stags' rutting season.

There came a day when, because of his familiarity with the deer and his belief in their inoffensiveness, Leveret was, quite literally, caught napping. He had made his couch in the softest, greenest area of grassland and, since he hadn't sought out his Farthing Wood comrades recently, he was quite unaware of the risks he was running as he lay amongst that choice verdure.

The sun was warm on his back, the air balmy; he slumbered peacefully. But a movement, a rustle of the grass and Leveret was instinctively awake. He opened his eyes. A huge white head bearing massive antlers confronted him. Leveret at first wasn't disturbed. Just another member of the deer herd, he thought. Then he noticed the stag's expression. It was not a friendly one.

Trey lowered his head and he scraped the ground with a front hoof as he looked at the hare. He looked like a bull about to charge. Leveret didn't wait to find out. He leapt up and bounded through the grasses. Trey galloped after him. He was in an ugly mood. This animal had ignored his ruling. He meant to punish him. The hare must be made an example to deter others. The stag crashed through the grassland area, flattening the succulent stalks he was so determined to save for the herd's sole enjoyment. Fleet of foot as Trey was, Leveret's elastic bounds left the deer farther and farther behind. The hare's constantly veering course was impossible to follow for long. At last, Trey pulled up. He tossed his head, half in frustration, half in bewilderment at Leveret's pace. But he was content that he had driven home his lesson. He didn't think Leveret would be back.

Trey was correct in his assumption. Leveret had been alarmed and frightened. He kept running and leaping long after the grassland was well behind him. He was a highly strung animal and so intent on flight that he almost collided with Friendly, Fox and Vixen's son, who was lapping listlessly from a puddle.

'Hey! Slow down! What's the hurry?' Friendly called out, cheerfully. 'It's too hot for racing.'

The well-known tones of the affectionate animal's voice halted Leveret's career. He turned, relieved to find a companion.

'Whatever's the matter?' Friendly asked. 'You look badly scared.'

Leveret brought his breath and racing heart under control before he attempted to answer. 'There's a mad creature amongst the deer herd,' he explained. He was still distressed. 'He *attacked* me. Charged at me, the great brute, while I was sleeping. A small animal like me! Without a word of warning. If it's some sort of stupid game. . . .'

Friendly recognized the culprit at once. 'Oh, you've encountered Trey, have you? The mighty new Lord of the Reserve!' He sounded contemptuous. 'No, Leveret, this is no game. Haven't you heard? This stag has set himself up as the successor to his great ancestor. Only he's not satisfied with dominating the deer herd. He wants all of us to pay him homage.'

'But – but – a deer?' Leveret spluttered. 'I thought we had nothing to fear from any of them. They've been our friends – allies even – in the old days.'

'Well, these are new days, Leveret. The old order, you see, has passed. And it seems we're to accept it – or go.'

5

Owl's Progress

Tawny Owl skimmed over the motorway to the open countryside again. Quietness enveloped him. Soon he felt hungry once more. He caught what he needed and ate, comfortably lodged in the fork of a tree. He was quite alone and he was beginning to enjoy it. He thought for a moment about his companions in White Deer Park but then quickly dismissed them from his mind. He was relishing his solitude, away from Weasel's carping comments and the young foxes' teasing that he had endured for too long. He looked forward to reaching his destination, to re-visiting the old haunts and, above all, to the awe in which he would be held as the only Farthing Wood creature to have dared to journey back. Just let those young foxes hear his story! They'd soon change their tune, especially when he arrived on the scene with the missing female they had loved to joke about.

Tawny Owl rested only briefly after eating. He was eager to press on. He felt fresh and full of energy. He flitted noiselessly through the moonlit summer night over the fox-hunting terrain where Vixen had so nearly lost her life. By dawn he was within sight of the river. An ancient hollow oak beckoned him to roost. He fluttered down and settled himself inside.

A short distance outside White Deer Park, Whistler was dutifully beginning his search for the errant Owl.

The next evening Tawny Owl crossed the river. Memories flooded back once again of Fox's accident in the water when he had been carried away downstream, away from his friends. But all that was ancient history. With the river behind him Owl travelled more circumspectly. He wasn't so sure of recognizing the route. Until he reached Farthing Wood itself, there would be no more prominent landmarks. However he *felt* his direction was correct. His instincts seemed to guide him. What didn't ring quite true was the ease with which he was travelling. Of course the journey of the animals from Farthing Wood to the Nature Reserve had been infinitely more difficult for land-travelling creatures, especially when the whole party had agreed to adapt its pace to accommodate the smallest representatives such as Toad, who had actively been demonstrating the route part of the time, and voles and fieldmice: tiny creatures who could only go in short stages. Up in the air, problems and barriers to progress that had seemed almost insurmountable on that journey, were as nothing.

The speed with which Tawny Owl covered the

distance surprised him more than anything. The long odyssey which he and his companions had undergone before had seemed at times as if it would never end. Now, alone, and flying at his own pace, it appeared that his journey would be completed in a matter of days. When he picked out from the air a certain copse whose shape was remarkably familiar, Tawny Owl felt he was indeed getting close. The copse was chiefly memorable for its rookery.

Tawny Owl glided in under cover of darkness and holed up in a dead elm. He meant to surprise the rooks by his presence when they awoke in the morning. Some of them would be bound to recognize him. As he had eaten on the way he allowed himself a semi-doze as he watched, fitfully, the gleaming stars begin to pale. But his doze was rudely interrupted.

The rooks began to call harshly and urgently at the first glimmer of daylight. They were not calls proclaiming territory or ownership but calls of alarm and warning. Still perched on their untidy nests of twigs they passed angry calls from one to another that echoed back and forth in the tree tops. Tawny Owl had been spied and he was not welcome. There were young still in the nests.

Owl clung uncertainly to the grey barkless branch of the stricken tree. He wasn't sure what to do. He supposed, in this murky light, he must seem to the rooks to be just another threatening predator. He decided to wait until the full light of day would reveal to them who it was who had come amongst them. The light grew but there was no lessening of the clamour. Indeed the calls became more raucous, more strident.

Eventually some of the angry birds left their nests and flew close to Owl in a mobbing action. They jeered at him, calling him offensive names such as murderer, robber and vandal. Owl was most put out. He tried to recognize amongst these rooks one who would have known him in the past. He and the Farthing Wood animals had spent a while in their copse and had been warmly welcomed by their hosts as heroes. But as he searched the faces with their long pointed beaks and glittering eyes he could see no hint of dawning friendliness in any of them. And they all looked the same. He couldn't have told them apart. Purple-black plumage with an iridescent sheen that reflected the early rays of the sun. Sharp, malevolent features. They span around him, deliberately malicious, hoping to rid their copse of his presence by their unremitting pressure.

'What, isn't there one of you who knows me?' Tawny Owl called out in bewilderment. 'Not one of you who knows the name of Farthing Wood?'

'Never heard of it.'

'No such place.'

'Farthing Wood? This is Rookery Copse. No other stand of woodland round here.'

Their voices screeched at him. They knew nothing of his past.

'Fox, Badger, Toad, Kestrel, Tawny Owl,' the besieged bird cried, desperately attempting to call himself to mind. 'We travelled here. Before. You made us welcome.'

'Welcome? Welcome? *They'd* be welcome, I don't think,' one screeched back.

'No friends of ours.'

'None of them!'

'But you must remember,' Tawny Owl almost pleaded. 'If not you, then your elders. Where are they?'

'What do you want with them? Leave them alone.'

'Get away from our copse!'

'Don't you see?' Tawny Owl wheedled. 'The older birds will recognize me. I was here before.'

They didn't want to hear. An owl was an enemy when young were in the nests. That's all they knew. They flew at him, buffeting him with their wings. They hoped to topple him from his perch. When that didn't work, the braver among them began aiming their beaks at him, stabbing downwards as they fluttered close. Tawny Owl gave ground. It was futile to resist any longer. Times were changed. There was no camaraderie to be looked for here. He flapped away from his branch and even then the rooks chased him, egged on by their success. They screamed their delight at his defeat, trying to make his retreat as humiliating as they could. The disappointed owl found himself putting on speed to rid himself of their deafening cries. At last they fell back, satisfied they had defended their nest sites with great daring.

Tawny Owl flew on dispiritedly. Now solitude didn't seem so attractive. He longed for some creature, animal or bird, to show him a jot of fellow feeling. He had lived for so long among friends he had forgotten what life was like in the usually hostile environment of nature. He thought of Bold, Fox's and Vixen's cub, who must have encountered just the same suspicion and enmity during his bid for independence away from the influence of his father. And what a hard time *he* had had of it. Owl put the thought behind him. The rooks' unpleasantness had tired him out, even frightened him a little. He needed to sleep and, first of all, to compose himself.

Without realizing it, Tawny Owl was flying back on himself, back in the direction from which he'd come to the copse. His one thought was to find a suitable perch. He didn't enjoy daylight very much except as a time to rest. He found a solitary hawthorn whose branches were almost impenetrable. Inside the thick canopy of greenery he could at last relax. The day passed him by and the few small songbirds who alighted on the thorn soon left again when they saw an owl hiding in its midst.

As usual Tawny Owl roused at dusk. He got himself airborne and immediately felt that he had been thrown off course. But he wanted to avoid the rookery at all costs, so he could not use the copse as a guide again. What he could do, however, was to use the noise of the rooks themselves as a clue. He knew that at dusk there was always a sort of concert of cawing as the birds settled themselves for the night. So he circled for a while until he picked up their sound. Congratulating himself on this brainwave, Tawny Owl flew towards the sound without ever getting too close to give himself trouble. The noise reached a crescendo and then gradually faded behind him and so Owl knew he had passed Rookery Copse and should soon be on the right track again. But it didn't prove as simple as that. He couldn't seem to get his bearings. In his mind he pictured an orchard, a marsh, a road and rows of houses. That was the way back if things were still as they had been before, but he found he couldn't locate any of these features. Then Tawny Owl berated himself for his stupidity. Of course things weren't the same as before. How could they be? All that time ago. . . .

He broke off his efforts at navigation to hunt. He decided he must then seek guidance. He caught himself a rat that was trying to raid a squirrels' drey. As he disposed of his prey it occurred to him that the squirrels might be able to help. He finished his meal. Then he flew back to the birch tree where the drey was sited. The tree grew alongside a couple of young oaks in a patch of undergrowth.

The squirrels at first scolded Tawny Owl for coming too close, just as they tried to warn off any predator from the youngsters they had to protect. But when the bird pointed out the good turn he had done them they quietened down and listened.

'Do you know a place called Farthing Wood?' Owl asked. 'It's not far from here.'

'Wood? There's no wood anywhere around here,' the mother squirrel replied. '*We'd* be living there if there were. . . .'

Tawny Owl sighed. The same reaction as from the rooks. 'But you must have heard of it, at least,' he suggested. 'There was woodland around here once. I used to live in it.'

'Doubtless there was,' the male squirrel conceded. 'But what's the use of asking us about a place that doesn't exist?'

'I only wanted to know if you'd heard the name,' Tawny Owl said. He decided he wouldn't tell them he was attempting to travel to a wood that they believed was non-existent.

The squirrels looked at each other. 'I've heard the name,' said the female. 'But not for a long time. I seem to recall there was some sort of tale attached to it.'

Tawny Owl perked up considerably. 'Yes, there was,' he said eagerly. 'I – I mean,' he added quickly, 'that I believe the tale would have been about how the inhabitants of the Wood had to leave it. Isn't that so?'

'Yes. Yes, that's it,' the squirrel answered. 'The wildlife all around here used to talk about them. Many of the older ones saw them pass. But they never knew for sure what happened to them.'

Tawny Owl was burning to tell the squirrels. But he fought the inclination down in order to pursue his main objective. With bated breath he asked: 'In which direction would Farthing Wood have been?'

The squirrels flicked their bushy tails as they pondered. 'It must have been,' the father squirrel said slowly, 'where the human dwellings have spread.'

'Yes, yes!' cried Tawny Owl. 'The men built over it, didn't they?' He was becoming excited.

'Well, if you know that, you must know where it was,' the squirrel rejoined in a puzzled way.

'But I haven't seen any human dwellings,' Tawny Owl spluttered. This was so exasperating!

'You can't have been over the hill then,' the female squirrel told him. 'They're all around there. Now then, if you have nothing further to bother us with, we'll go back to our rest.'

'Nothing more, nothing more,' Tawny Owl called. He was already in the air.

'Thank you again for the rat-killing,' the father squirrel cried generously. 'We really are –'

But Tawny Owl was away. He saw where the land began to rise and followed it directly. At the top of the little hill he looked over and there, below, were the bright lights of human habitations and streets.

'So!' he breathed to himself. 'I'm home.'

But he wasn't. Not quite.

6

Water Rights

Whistler the heron abandoned his search when it was obvious that Tawny Owl had left the immediate environs of White Deer Park. 'I'll keep a look-out for him from time to time,' he told himself. 'But I can't go combing the entire countryside.' On his return he flew along the length of the stream and was distressed at what he found there. At intervals there were dead bodies of small creatures, mainly watervoles, lying either on the banks or at the edge of the water, bobbing on the ripples. There was a pair of coots who had suffered the same fate. Their deserted nest amongst some reeds had two fairly well-grown, but lifeless, youngsters in it.

'This is terrible,' Whistler said. 'I wonder what's caused this?'

He flew up and down, peering at the water for any sign that would give an explanation. But he could see

nothing unusual. Later he noticed Adder and Sinuous
sunning themselves in their favourite spot. These days
they were always together. Whistler wasn't sure if he
should disturb them but he guessed Adder had seen
him so he decided in the end to fly over.

'Have you found anything?' Adder enquired without
much interest. He knew Whistler had been looking for
Tawny Owl.

Whistler mistook him. 'Have you seen them too?' he
asked, referring to the dead creatures.

Adder looked at him curiously. 'Them?' he repeated.
'You don't mean to say. . . .' He was picturing Tawny
Owl flying back in triumph with his consort.

'Bodies,' Whistler said. 'By the stream. A number of
them.'

'I told you so,' Sinuous remarked to her companion.
Whistler waited politely for an explanation.

'She thinks the place has become one of menace,' the
snake said. 'Ever since the Great Stag pegged out
there.' He was never one to show overmuch respect.

'I'm not the only one who thinks so. Most of you are
steering well clear of the area,' Sinuous said to the
heron.

'Yes. Except those who live on its fringes,' he said.
'But now it seems they're at risk. I don't know how long
those bodies have been there. *I* haven't been near the
stream for a long while.'

Adder ventured a quip. 'When Whistler the heron
ceases to patrol the stream's banks there's something
fishy going on.'

Whistler chuckled. 'That's just it, Adder. There *are*
no fish.'

Now Adder was serious. He had remembered Toad. 'Best to leave the place well alone,' he said. 'I wish I'd seen Toad. He sometimes swims there.'

Whistler was surprised at his words. The snake didn't often commit himself to pangs of anxiety. 'The land is damp and humid enough for him at present, I hope,' said the heron. 'And he does spend a lot of time with his friends the frogs in the Pond, I believe?'

'He's a great traveller, our Toad,' said Adder. 'Nobody knows that better than I. There's no knowing where he might turn up.'

'He must look out for himself then, mustn't he?' Sinuous observed primly. She was well aware of the little clique of Farthing Wood animals who continued to concern themselves about each other. The idea bored her as she wasn't party to it.

'I think I'll look out for him as well,' Adder lisped, 'if you've no objection?'

Toad was actually nowhere in the vicinity of the stream. He was enjoying the bonanza of grubs, worms and insects that was all around him. He was a very plump Toad indeed. Swimming wasn't on his mind very much and, in common with his friends, he hadn't much desire at present to visit the stream. The Edible Frogs around the Pond didn't see much of him either. However, they did see a lot of other creatures. Many of the Park's inhabitants were using the Pond as their chief drinking place now. Amongst these were the White Deer themselves as well as those members of the Farthing Wood community who ranged most widely, such as the younger foxes. So it was only a matter of time before one of them was confronted by Trey.

The young fox Plucky, still barely more than a cub, had his grandfather Bold's liking for roaming far afield. As soon as he was big enough he began to acquaint himself with every corner of the Nature Reserve. It happened one day he was drinking at the Pond when Trey arrived. Trey was suspicious. He knew there were no fox-holes anywhere near the Pond.

'What quarter of the Park do you come from?' Trey demanded.

'None in particular,' Plucky answered him coolly.

'This Pond is the deer herd's drinking place,' Trey announced.

'Yes, it's very convenient, isn't it?' Plucky remarked. 'I believe a lot of animals use it.'

'Do they indeed? We'll see about that,' the stag responded. 'The deer herd needs to have a constant supply of the freshest water. This Pond was always intended as our water-hole. So I'm reserving it for our exclusive use.'

Plucky looked at him in amazement. 'But, surely, it's big enough for every creature to use who wants to?' he questioned.

'Maybe not if we should have a long dry spell,' Trey replied. 'Anyway, you smaller animals can make do with any odd puddle. You don't need the quantity of water a fully-grown deer needs. And there are many of us.'

Plucky knew about the Great Stag. 'If what you say is true, why did your father drink at the stream?'

'He was a creature of habit,' Trey answered. 'He

preferred to drink from running water. And he wasn't my father. Our relationship was very distant.'

'Grandfather perhaps? You resemble him a good deal.'

'No. I'm nothing like him – as you'll find out.' Trey sounded angry and threatening. 'He was always too tolerant of lesser creatures,' he added scornfully.

Plucky was in no way abashed. He simply stared back at the beast, then finished quenching his thirst. As he ambled away the stag called after him: 'Remember what I've said.'

Plucky did. And he remembered to tell all his relatives, too. The seniors, Fox and Vixen, were already incensed by the incident with Leveret. This was the last straw.

'We won't take this lying down,' Fox said grimly. 'Who does this creature think he is, dictating to us?'

'He'll put himself in a false position,' Vixen commented. 'He doesn't speak for the rest of the herd. The hinds are as friendly as ever.'

'He's talking poppycock,' Fox declared. 'He must have a small mind if he thinks he can push ideas like this on to us. We must all meet and work out our course of action. Plucky, I want you to take the word round. The Hollow. Dusk tomorrow.'

The next night the Farthing Wood elders assembled in their traditional meeting place. Plucky had gathered them all. He knew just where to find each one. Badger, Weasel, Whistler, Adder and Toad had obeyed the summons. Leveret and Mossy were there, as were Fox and Vixen's offspring Friendly and Charmer together with others of their relatives. Plucky was the youngest animal present. The fox clan was the most numerous. They were also the most daring and skilful of the animals. But of the original band of travellers, only Tawny Owl was absent.

'We all know the situation,' Fox began. 'The question is, what are we going to do about it?'

'Just as you said before, Fox,' Weasel replied. 'Call Trey's bluff. What can he do? He can't deal with all of us. We're too many and too scattered.'

'I've seen what he can do,' Leveret spoke up. 'He'll wreak his will on the more vulnerable of us.'

'We can't allow that,' said Friendly. 'He'll find he's got too many enemies to handle.'

'What could you do, Friendly?' asked his mate Russet. 'Attack him?'

'No, he's too powerful,' Friendly admitted. 'But we can outwit him. My father is the shrewdest, wiliest animal in the Park. He's more than a match for the wits of Trey.'

'Thank you, Friendly,' said Fox. 'One plan has occurred to me and it's one that wouldn't actually involve any of us. Not directly, anyhow.' Every eye was on him expectantly. 'We need a champion,' he announced.

'A – champion?' Toad echoed. 'A champion what?'

'A champion fool, I should think,' drawled Adder, 'if he tries to meddle with that creature.'

'You don't understand, Adder,' said Fox. 'I'm not talking about one of us.'

'Do I perceive, Fox, that your thoughts lie amongst

the other stags in the herd?' Whistler asked in his old-fashioned way.

'Exactly that. You've guessed it, old friend. We need to find someone who'll challenge him.'

'How do we do that?' Badger wanted to know. 'Trey already seems to have cowed them all into submission.'

'No, no, Badger, not really,' Fox answered. 'He only assumes he has. They're content to leave him well alone at the moment. But it won't be like that at the rut. Don't you remember how the Great Stag himself had to fight to keep command at those times?'

'Do you have anyone in mind as our ch-champion?' Mossy stammered. He was a little overawed by all the bigger animals present.

'Not yet,' Fox replied. 'But I mean to do a bit of scouting around.'

'Sort of – look over the material?' joked Toad.

'Sort of.' Fox grinned. 'It may be I can drop a hint here and there.' He put his head on one side. 'Perhaps,' he considered, 'we can all help. Stir a few of them up. You know, set them on. We might have quite a few champions at the end of it all.'

'I still think he could defeat all comers,' Leveret said pessimistically. He laid his long ears flat against his back. 'He's a mighty figure.'

'I think you're right,' agreed Fox, 'if it were to be one by one. But what if they should take him on together?'

'Deer never fight like that,' Vixen reasoned. 'We can't change their nature, my dearest.'

There was a long silence. Then Fox said: 'I obviously need to do some more thinking. But in the meantime a word in an ear here and there. . . .'

'They may listen to you foxes,' said Adder, 'but what message is so important that these stags are likely to give attention to a toad or a snake or a mole?' He looked at Mossy so disdainfully that the little animal quailed, not because he was a coward – he was far from that – but because he felt so insignificant.

'Well, that's straightforward enough,' Fox answered. 'You simply tell them that Trey intends to drive all rivals from the Park.'

7

Farthinghurst

Tawny Owl was bewildered. There were just so many buildings! They were all big and frightening and their myriad lights dazzled him. It was a long time since he had come so close to a mass of human dwellings and now he began to ask himself why he had come here. His original reason for leaving White Deer Park was quite different to the one that had spurred him on to re-visit his old home and birthplace. He hadn't found that suitable companion during his flight across country. And now, as he viewed from the wing this man-built sprawl, he knew there was certainly no likelihood of any owl being found in its alien landscape.

'Can that really be where Farthing Wood once flourished?' he murmured to himself. 'Or have I, after all, taken the wrong direction?'

No, the squirrels had been quite specific. Well, there was no use his expecting to recognize any feature in that conglomeration. Certainly not by night when the artificial lights blazed so confusingly.

'I may take a close look in the daylight,' Tawny Owl said. 'It's just possible there's something down there that'll trigger a reaction in my poor old brain. I can't turn tail now without making sure.'

He needed to find somewhere to roost. But where? He didn't want to go back to the few trees where the squirrels had built their drey. He examined the nearest gardens below. There were trees in them – for ornamentation – but such puny, immature saplings could only provide cover and support for the smallest of birds. The buildings were mostly in tall blocks and these were flat-roofed so there was no chance of Owl tucking himself away in a sheltered corner or in the lee of a chimney-stack. The smaller buildings had sloping roofs. There was nothing to perch on amongst those. But he did notice one of them had a gaping and invitingly dark entrance hole, like an open mouth, high up on one side of its roof. There were no lights there. All the lights in that house were much lower down and well away from the hole which left it in undisturbed darkness and privacy. Tawny Owl was sorely tempted to hide himself in there until dawn. But could he be sure it was quite safe?

He flew down closer to the building. It certainly seemed quiet enough. Following the slope of the roof he fluttered awkwardly until he was able to perch at the opening itself. Although he didn't know it his talons were resting on the window-ledge of an open attic window. He shuffled along it and peered inside. His feet made scuffling noises but they didn't seem to have caused any disturbance. He waited awhile. The room was quiet and bare except for a long wall of shelving filled with books. Tawny Owl saw the racks as potential perching posts. After a few moments he entered the room and fluttered across to its far end. On the top shelf of the book racks there was a perfect gap between two rows of volumes which was just wide enough for Owl to wedge himself comfortably in. He settled himself but remained wakeful.

For some time noises were detectable underneath this converted loft – human noises. But to Tawny Owl they seemed distant enough to be overlooked. Eventually they ceased. The night sky grew darker as he watched. All over the estate lights were being switched off as the human community retired to rest. The bird waited patiently for dawn.

As the night wore on a breeze began to blow into the room. Half-awake, half-asleep, Tawny Owl shifted his feet and ruffled his feathers. The breeze stiffened. The open window began to swing gently to and fro. Tawny Owl couldn't foresee the danger. The wind strengthened steadily and, now blowing directly against the window, pushed it gradually back, closing the gap and thus the owl's escape route a fraction at a time. Tawny Owl recognized his danger all too late. As he hurled himself from the shelf in a frantic bid to squeeze through the narrowing outlet, a particularly strong gust finally slammed the window shut. Tawny Owl's head and wings were battered against the glass and he dropped to the floor stunned.

It was broad day when he recovered. He struggled to his feet and fluttered up to the inside sill. The window was fast closed. He looked out on a scene of alarming activity; alarming because it was human. Cars and other vehicles moved along the network of roads. People seemed to be everywhere – walking, standing, working in their gardens. Children and dogs were running about. Cats sunned themselves in patches of warmth, oblivious of everything including the watching owl, trapped in a garret.

What was he to do? He began to inspect the room. The first thing he noticed which had not been apparent in the pitch dark was that the loft door stood ajar. Was there some other way out for him? Noises in the lower part of the building reminded him that this door was also the way in to the roost he had so foolishly chosen, for any creature, human or otherwise, who lived underneath. He gulped nervously and sought his night perch, feeling more secure between the tightly-stacked books as if in some way they might protect him.

Time drifted past to the accompaniment of human sounds, inside and outside, which deterred the poor bird from making any rash movement. He was both hungry and thirsty. There was dust everywhere and Tawny Owl felt as if a quantity of it had lodged in his throat. Well, he couldn't stay there indefinitely. The window wasn't going to open of its own accord so he must try the other way. He needed to muster up some of that old Farthing Wood spirit: the spirit of adventure. Tawny Owl stretched himself and preened his feathers. He looked towards the door. He was trying to steel himself for action. The noise from beneath increased in volume. He sank back. After all, he told himself, there was no point in taking unnecessary risks. He would wait until the house grew quiet.

But it didn't grow quiet. In fact the bird soon became aware of something approaching his secret hidey-hole. There were footfalls – soft, cautious footfalls like those of a creature who might be exploring new territory. Tawny Owl kept his great eyes trained on the door. It was difficult for him to keep still as the regular pad – pad – pad of feet approached ever nearer. He tensed, ready for flight.

A black cat came into the room and paused, just inside the door. It raised one paw uncertainly and sniffed the air. Its head turned slowly to Tawny Owl's end of the room. It wasn't a large cat and the bird tried to tell himself it could pose no threat to an owl. But his efforts were unavailing. He was well and truly alarmed for the consequences if he should be discovered. He remained as still as he could, hoping he blended in with his incongruous surroundings. It was an absurd hope. The cat had sensed something was in the room and was systematically searching for it.

'Ah – there you are,' she said as her eyes alighted on the forlorn owl. 'I knew you were here somewhere.'

'I – I'm just leaving,' Tawny Owl hooted ineptly.

'I don't think you can,' the cat, who had noticed the window was closed, replied. 'How did you get in here?'

'Flew in – how do you think?' the bird blustered.

The cat sat down and regarded him coolly. 'You're not making much sense,' she said at length. 'How long have you been here?'

'Since the night. I meant to leave at dawn but –'

'You can't fly through glass,' the cat finished for him.

Tawny Owl was silent. Was the cat playing with him?

'You won't be able to stay here, you know,' the cat resumed. 'This isn't an aviary.'

'I don't want to stay here,' Tawny Owl declared. 'But how do I get out? Can you show me?'

The cat considered. 'I don't know about that,' she answered. 'You see, I'm supposed to be responsible for vermin. There was a problem with mice here. Up until recently. It took me quite a time to round them all up. But they're all gone now. I don't know if you'd be classed as vermin?'

Tawny Owl gaped at the implied insult and now he was angry. 'How dare you!' he screeched. 'Vermin indeed! I am an owl. I *hunt* vermin. I *eat* vermin. I – I –'

'All right,' the cat said smoothly. 'I get the message. You're not vermin. But I may still have to come after you.'

Tawny Owl's anger saved him. His temper was up. 'Try me!' he cried. He flexed his talons. His huge eyes glared at the cat's presumption. He was exasperated that he couldn't open his wings to their full span. That would have shaken the animal.

The black cat stared at the bird, in particular at his talons. She was weighing up her chances. She began to see that this was no ordinary bird.

'Sooty! Sooty!' a child's voice called from below. The cat's attention wavered. 'Sooty! Are you there?' The cat turned away. The child was mounting the stairs.

Tawny Owl heard these new footsteps in great alarm. He wanted nothing to do with humans. They were unpredictable and beyond a wild creature's understanding. He didn't know whether to stay put or make a dash for the open doorway. The cat had temporarily forgotten his existence as she waited for the child to appear.

'Soo – ty, Soo – ty,' the shrill voice chanted, ever louder as its owner neared the top stair. The cat miaowed, raising her black tail as she saw her seeker.

'There you are!' cried the child triumphantly. A little red-haired boy of about six years came into the room, stooping to give his pet a cuddle. The cat pushed herself against his legs affectionately and nuzzled his eager hands.

Tawny Owl guessed there was no threat to him here and decided it was his best opportunity for escape. He fluttered off the bookshelf, causing the startled boy to scream, and swooped over his head through the doorway, banking sharply to make the tight turn down the staircase. The bird had no idea where he was heading, but was intent on finding the first available opening to the outside world.

The boy's scream had already stirred the rest of the household. Now he was calling out in the utmost excitement from upstairs. 'Daddy, a bird! A bird in the loft!'

The father came running from below. Tawny Owl had skimmed down the first flight of stairs and reached the landing of the first storey. Bedroom doors were open here and Owl lunged for the first entrance he saw and flew straight for the window. A girl shrieked as his wings clipped her face as she sat at her dressing-table. Fooled by the gleamingly clean picture window which appeared to the bird to be open air, Tawny Owl almost crashed against the glass but managed to swerve at the last moment. The confined space of the bedroom was difficult to negotiate. The girl was adding her cries to the small boy's. It was enough to terrify any wild animal and now the father arrived on the scene, believing his children were being attacked. He saw the great bird and, instinctively protective, tried to knock it to the floor. Tawny Owl veered from right to left and back again to avoid the man's flailing arms. Surprisingly the girl came to his aid.

'Don't hit him, Dad, please,' she begged. 'He just wants to get out. Open the window!'

The man ran to the window. Now Tawny Owl had more room. He flapped through the door and continued along the landing. He ignored the other open doorways, having learnt his lesson. He came to another staircase and followed it down. Now he was in the hall. The front door was closed. He fluttered to the floor and tried to gain breath. His head was in a whirl. But the man and his children, together with the cat, were in hot pursuit. Tawny Owl didn't understand their intentions. He struggled on again into a room leading off to the right. It was full of furniture – fearsome obstacles for Owl. But what he saw ahead of him made his heart leap. An open window!

It was a small window – a fanlight – left on the latch. But he was determined to squeeze through it even if it should mean leaving some of his feathers. He reached the latch and perched on it. He saw the opening was even tighter than he had feared. As the family came into the room, all talking at the tops of their voices and pointing at him, Tawny Owl pushed his head outside.

The feel of the wind on his face, added to the din behind him, encouraged him onwards. His talons grappled the latch. He pushed and thrust his body through the gap. He felt the hard edges of the window gripping his sides, pinching him like a sort of vice. But he refused to give up. A little more discomfort and, with a final heave, he popped out of the window like a cork out of a bottle.

Instantly he soared upwards despite his throbbing sides, enjoying the supreme luxury of spreading his wings in the free fresh air; in unobstructed and limitless space. He looked around him as he rose higher in the air. Human faces pressed against the glass, watching his progress in admiration, almost in envy. Envy of the supreme freedom of the flight of a bird.

The man said: 'That's the first time an owl has been seen in Farthinghurst. You must remember this, children.'

'And he chose us to visit,' said the girl. 'Look, here are some of his feathers.'

Tawny Owl flew on. Hunger and thirst were forgotten as he flew over the houses, the blocks of flats, the shops. For he knew now that beneath him was what was once Farthing Wood. Its soil, its plants, its roots lay under this man-made wilderness of concrete and brick and metal. And he knew it was Farthing Wood because there was just one remnant of it still existing. The remnant was a tree: a solitary, isolated but massive beech. Tawny Owl had recognized it at once as its great sweeping branches beckoned to him like welcoming arms which longed to draw him into their lonely embrace. This great beech, which now straddled the boundaries of two identical plots on the estate and therefore belonged to nobody, was the very same beech which had served as a meeting-point for the animals of Farthing Wood as they had embarked on their hazardous journey. It was from beneath this very tree, that now enfolded Tawny Owl in its rich greenery, that their long trek had begun. And this was all that the industrious humans and their machines had allowed to stand of Farthing Wood.

8

Holly

The beech's generous cover hid Tawny Owl for the rest of the day. He didn't dare to venture forth again even to moisten his parched mouth. He waited. And he thought.

He thought of his carefree days in Farthing Wood before the humans had come, when he had been so much younger. He thought of the other creatures who had lived there who had become his travelling companions first and then his trusted friends. What feelings would they experience were they to join him at the Great Beech now? How their world had changed! Yet, oddly enough, Owl didn't feel sentimental about his old home. That life was too far back in the past. He found himself thinking more about White Deer Park. He was surprised at himself. And what surprised him most of all was that he actually felt homesick for it.

By twilight Tawny Owl had come to the conclusion

that he had made a mistake coming to this place. It was barren. Barren of hunting opportunities and barren of company. When he felt ready for it he would begin the flight back. In the meantime his ordeal in the house had exhausted him and he needed to get his strength back.

Under cover of darkness he sought water. A garden pond soon provided him with that. Food, however, would be a problem. Then he remembered what the black cat had said about mice. So there must be prey to be caught somewhere in the area. Of course, mice inside a house were no use to an owl. But mice got into human dwellings from outside and so in that case, thought Owl, there would be others to find.

'And if anyone can find mice,' he told himself again, '*I* can.' So he began to search the gardens; along the fence bottoms, around the sheds, under the hedges. And pretty soon he found them all right. And he also found he wasn't the only one hunting them. From time to time he caught a glimpse of another bird swooping in the darkness, never very close, always keeping its distance. And he heard the squeals of mice *he* hadn't caught, just a few garden plots away from where he was intent on his own quest.

Each time Tawny Owl made a kill he took it back to the beech and ate in seclusion on one of the broad grey branches. He wondered where the other hunter perched to eat. He didn't know that in between his visits to the tree the second bird was using it as well. Finally their trips coincided. Each was aware there was another occupant in a separate part of the tree. Tawny Owl wondered what sort of bird was sharing his roosting site. As it was a nocturnal hunter like himself he had every reason to suppose it was another owl. He was curious. But the other bird spoke first.

'How long have you been hunting this area?'

Tawny Owl swivelled round in excitement. The voice belonged to a female. 'That depends on how you look at it,' he answered.

'What do you mean?'

'It means that I know the area as well as any living creature and better than most,' he explained grandly. 'But I've been absent for a long while.'

'Then you can't know it as well as you think,' came the reply. 'The area has been steadily changing ever since I can remember.'

'You don't have to tell me,' Tawny Owl said, very much on his dignity. 'I know all about Farthing Wood, believe you me.'

'I believe you,' said the other owl. 'But do you know about Farthinghurst?'

'Farthinghurst?'

'Yes, that's the name of this area now. Farthing Wood is long gone.'

'I can see that!' Tawny Owl exclaimed irritably. 'But, did you know that we are now perching in a part of it?'

'Oh yes. I've known and used this tree for several seasons. I think it's always been here.'

'As long as the Wood itself. And now it's all that remains.'

The owl was intrigued. 'How do you know so much?'

'If you're a good listener, I've a long story to tell you. But for the moment, suffice to say that Farthing Wood was my home from the day I hatched. When its destruction was imminent I left. And now, as you see, I've returned.'

'I don't pretend to understand your reasons,' said the other owl, 'since your Wood has now disappeared.'

'Ah – that's another matter,' Tawny Owl told her. 'But what about you? Is this your permanent territory? Tell me about yourself.'

'Not much to tell.' The female owl fluttered to a closer branch. She was another Tawny. 'I was hatched on the fringes of the Wood amidst the roar of men's machinery. There was just a tiny patch of woodland then but, from what you say, I think it may once have been much larger. Most of my kin were killed or found other territories. I stayed around, though.'

'Why?'

'Simple. Abundant food. In my early days there was almost a plague of mice who came in from the countryside to raid the humans' buildings. They were attracted originally by a great barn where grain was stored. This was on the edge of the estate. From there they spread all over, getting into the humans' own dwelling-places. So there was never a shortage of prey for me. Of course, the humans got to work to eradicate my food supply. But they could never quite winkle out every last mouse. So I've hung on here. I compete with cats and others but I've never starved. I suppose I've been lazy in some ways.'

'Far from it,' Tawny Owl contended. 'It always makes sense to exploit a constant source of food. And where do you roost?'

'Well – right here, of course. Where else is there?'

'Here? But I was sheltering here myself during the day. I didn't realize. . . .'

'No reason why you should. I saw you, but you were, by all appearances, oblivious of everything.'

'I was exhausted,' Tawny Owl explained. Then he told her about his adventure in the loft.

'That was an error on your part, to go inside a man-dwelling,' the female owl asserted. 'I've learnt to steer well clear of them.'

'You're right, of course,' he agreed. 'But that was nothing compared to my previous adventures.'

'Oh? And when am I to have the privilege of hearing about them?'

'Any time you wish,' Tawny Owl promised. He was eager to impress. 'What do you call yourself?'

'I don't call myself anything,' she answered. 'And there's no-one else around to give me a name. At least,' she added, 'not until now. Perhaps you'd like to think of one for me?'

'Well, I – I don't know if I'm much good at that sort of thing,' he said awkwardly. 'But I'll try.'

'Do you have a name?'

'Yes. Tawny Owl,' he said.

'I can see that.' The female owl was amused. 'But what of your own individual name?'

'Well, that *is* it.' He rustled his wings. 'I've never needed another. My friends always called me that. I was the only owl in the party, you see.'

'Party?' she queried. 'No, I don't see.'

'I think I'd better tell you my story,' he said.

'I wish you would.'

So Tawny Owl related the story of the Animals of Farthing Wood and of their long journey to a new safe home. His companion was an avid listener. She was

thrilled and awed by his descriptions of the adventures
they had encountered on the way, so much so that she
wasn't absolutely sure whether he might not be
embellishing some of them. But he wasn't, of course.
He didn't have any need of embellishments. She hardly
spoke a word until he had finished. 'A thrilling tale
indeed,' she said. 'And so you all made your homes in
White Deer Park?'

'Yes, we did. And soon I shall return there.'

'Forgive me, but I don't understand why you ever
left it?'

'Aha,' Tawny Owl returned. 'That's quite another
story.'

The female owl didn't press him. She was beginning
to feel drowsy. She said, 'It seems so strange for a bird
to have mammals as his closest companions – and even
a reptile, too. I never heard of such a thing.'

'They've been true comrades, all of them,' he said.
He had got himself into quite an emotional state during
the recounting of his story, even to the point of being
prepared to forgive Weasel his teasing. 'Don't you ever
get lonely?'

'I hadn't thought about it before,' she answered.
'But now I see the advantage of friends in times of
difficulty.'

'I – er – could be a friend, you know,' Tawny Owl
offered hopefully.

'Well, I think maybe you already are,' she replied.
'And so really I think you must give me a name.'

'Yes, yes, now let me think . . . I have it!' he cried
suddenly. 'I shall call you Holly.'

'Holly! Why?'

'Because it's a good name for an owl,' he answered promptly. 'And besides – I can't think of anything else.'

She was not displeased. 'Holly, Holly,' she repeated, testing the name. 'Yes, I rather think I like it. It's nice to be called something.'

Tawny Owl was thoroughly pleased with himself. Now his thoughts took another turn and he felt glad he had come this far, after all. He hardly dared to hope that all his plans would be fulfilled. Yet Fate had brought him to this tree, the symbol of Farthing Wood, and here he had found Holly, its last survivor. There had to be some meaning to it all. His thoughts were interrupted.

'Where did you roost last?' she was asking.

'Here – on this very branch.'

'Then I shall join you there,' she said purposefully. And she flew over. 'We may as well start as we mean to go on, don't you think?' she added, perching by his side. 'Friends must stick together, mustn't they?'

9

A Rival in the Air

So the two birds roosted together in the beech tree during daylight. At night they hunted mice together. This became the pattern of Tawny Owl's new life and he had no complaints for the moment. He still intended to return to White Deer Park and, of course, he intended to take Holly along with him. But she seemed so content with her lot that he hesitated to broach the subject, fearing she might decline. In this he was quite wrong. Holly had of necessity lived a solitary life. Now she was enjoying the change and would not have wanted to be left alone again. She was a clever bird and also a little cunning. She knew Tawny Owl wanted her to stay with him; she guessed easily enough that he lacked a mate and she took this to be because of his age. From that it was simple enough to surmise that he would be keen to keep her and would therefore be willing to do her bidding. So she decided to make use of this situation. And, first of all, she would test his feelings towards her.

'I don't think you'll be going back to your Nature Reserve,' she remarked to him coyly one evening as they rested from hunting.

'I certainly shall,' he asserted.

'When will it be?'

Tawny Owl shuffled his feet. 'I – er – I'm not quite sure,' he answered.

'Why leave? Aren't you happy here?' Holly asked next.

'Up to a point, yes,' he had to say.

'We have an abundance of food, we have shelter, haven't we?'

'Yes, but you see, I don't feel this is my home any more. How could I? I belong in White Deer Park.'

'Then why did you come here?'

'I didn't plan to – at first,' he answered.

'What changed your mind?'

'Oh well, I'd already flown a considerable distance away from the Reserve and it occurred to me I might as well come a little further and see what the old place looked like. And, until recently, I wished I hadn't.'

Holly knew perfectly well what he was alluding to. But she pretended otherwise. 'I wonder why you changed your opinion?' she mused.

'Oh, you know,' he said gruffly.

'Do I?' she asked with feigned innocence.

'Well, I had hoped you understood,' Tawny Owl said. 'I mean, most creatures like company of a sort.'

'But weren't you telling me you had plenty of

company in the Park? Your friends the fox and the badger. . . .' She was making it difficult for him.

'Of course,' he said. He shifted up and down. Then he mumbled, 'But one always prefers company of one's own kind.'

'Ah. I see,' said Holly. 'How flattering,' she added softly. Then, 'How important is it to you?'

'Very,' he confessed.

'Then I ought to tell you something. You may lose my company.'

'How? Why?' Tawny Owl blustered.

'I think you may have a rival for it.'

'A rival? Oh, that's of no consequence. He'd soon quit the field when he saw I was around,' Tawny Owl told her self-importantly. He – the Farthing Wood Owl!

'You may be right, I can't tell,' Holly said. She wished to appear impartial. 'But – forgive me for saying it – he seems a much younger bird than yourself. I think I should warn you.'

Tawny Owl's self-esteem was rocked a little by this news. He wondered whether fame alone would be enough to ward off any challenge. And then, if the owl should be really young, would he have heard of the Owl from Farthing Wood? After all, Holly hadn't seemed aware of his status.

'Where have you seen this bird?' he asked cautiously.

Holly thought hard. The story was all invention. How could she make it seem convincing? 'Oh, I've seen him around for a long while,' she answered airily. 'He flits about in the distance, over the house-tops and along the hedge-plants. Sometimes he comes right by our roost and looks up inquisitively. He watches me, you know. I was aware of his presence before you arrived.'

'*I've* never seen him,' Tawny Owl declared. 'But I'll look out for him from now on!' He sounded determined. In fact he wasn't at all sure he believed her. Holly, however, was pleased with his reaction.

The next time they hunted together Tawny Owl really kept his eyes peeled for the slightest sign. He saw nothing large enough in the air to be an owl. When they were back on their perch he questioned his companion. Had she seen anything?

'Oh yes. He was around,' she told him with the greatest composure.

'But he couldn't have been!' Tawny Owl remonstrated. 'I looked everywhere.' He was becoming suspicious.

'You have to know where to look,' Holly pointed out. 'And besides, he's probably wary of you.'

This remark boosted Owl's ego. It was meant as a compliment and he took it as such. Holly's subtlety had dispelled his doubts for the time being. He didn't mention the other bird again but waited for her to do so. And she did.

Each night she pretended to have seen it, sometimes in one place, sometimes in another. And, according to her, this other male on occasion still flew close to the beech tree while they were resting.

'Not much of a rival, is he?' Tawny Owl remarked sarcastically. 'He never dares to show his face.'

Holly saw she might have miscalculated. She had to retrieve the situation. 'I'm so afraid he's just looking for his opportunity,' she said. 'When you're asleep, for instance. You always doze off long before I do.'

'Do I indeed?' Tawny Owl returned grumpily. He never liked to be reminded of his tendency to drowsiness. 'Well, I tell you what then. In future I'll stay awake and wait for him.'

For the next few days he did just that. He made a supreme effort to keep his eyes open although a full stomach always made him feel sleepy. He stared through the mass of branches until long after dawn when the beech gradually took on its colours of leaf green and silver grey.

'I saw nothing and nobody,' he kept telling her.

'I think he's waiting till your guard is down,' was Holly's answer. 'He's so clever.'

Tawny Owl was tiring of this game. He decided to bring it to a conclusion. 'Oh yes, he's clever all right,' he said. 'He's so clever at eluding me he's as good as invisible.'

'Oh, Tawny Owl,' responded Holly archly. 'Do you doubt me?'

Owl was sorely tempted to say so but refrained. 'No, no,' he lied. 'Why should I? But I mean to see off this interloper once and for all. So the next time you see him, you tell me straight away where he is and I'll get after him and drive him off.'

Holly was excited. 'Would you? Would you really?' she asked.

'Just see if I don't,' he answered grimly, but inwardly he smiled. He wondered how she would manage the affair.

That night Holly didn't see the elusive bird. Tawny

Owl's inward smile broadened. The next night and the night after that were the same. Owl was beside himself with glee. But Holly was deliberately lulling him into a state of unpreparedness. On the fourth night, as they skimmed together over the gardens searching for mice, he was on the point of remarking that his rival seemed to have given up when she suddenly startled him with cries of: 'There he is! There he is!'

Tawny Owl nearly plummeted to earth in his astonishment, but managed to correct his flight to save himself. 'Where?' he gasped breathlessly.

'There, look! Do you see where those new man-dwellings are being built?' She indicated by changing direction.

'Yes, I – I think I do.'

'He's skulking over there!' she screeched. Her cries were so convincingly raucous that for a moment Tawny Owl almost believed he could himself make out something in the distance. Did he see a fluttering figure?

'Quickly!' Holly urged him. 'He'll be gone.'

Now there was no choice for him. He had to fall in with her plan or appear cowardly. He flapped his wings hastily, increasing his speed, and zoomed towards his objective. Holly watched him with satisfaction.

Tawny Owl was really flying fast. He hoped that if a rival were around the bird would be frightened off by his purposefulness. But there was no rival around and Tawny Owl blundered straight into some almost invisible netting that flapped in the breeze, entangling himself and landing with a thump on a partially laid and unhardened concrete driveway that the netting had been erected to protect. As he struggled to free himself from the nylon mesh his talons and wings became daubed with gouts of thick wet cement mix. He got himself into the air. Now he knew very well there had been no other owl. He was furious with Holly for playing games with him. As yet he didn't realize the full extent of the plight he was in. He only knew his wing feathers were tacky and uncomfortable and that he couldn't move them as he wished. He felt strangely out of balance as if one side of his body was heavier than the other and it was most difficult for him to steer the course he wanted. He lumbered awkwardly back to Holly who had just pounced on a mouse.

'You can bring that back to the roost for *me*!' Tawny Owl cried imperiously. 'I've done your bidding and look at my reward.' He exhibited his cement-coated talons. 'I'll do no more hunting tonight – neither of mouse nor owl!' He bumbled his way to the beech in a sort of zigzag motion. He found it impossible to fly straight. He landed with extreme awkwardness, his plastered claws encumbering his ability to perch safely.

Holly obediently brought him her most recent kill. She thought he deserved it. She didn't understand his predicament yet and believed Tawny Owl was only grumpy because he had soiled his plumage when he fell.

'You and your stupid stories!' he berated her. 'There never was another owl, was there?'

Holly replied by meekly laying the dead mouse within his reach.

Tawny Owl was hungry and tore mouthfuls off the carcass so that he could continue his tirade in between swallowing. Usually he disposed of a mouse whole. 'I don't know what fun you've been having at my expense,' he snapped, 'but I can tell you it's over. No doubt you think there's no fool' – gulp – 'like an old fool but you'll find out that Tawny' – gulp – 'Owl from Farthing Wood is nobody's fool!'

'Oh, it's not a game,' said Holly. 'You've got me all wrong.' She looked at him with her huge round eyes. 'I only wanted to tell if you were in earnest about me and our keeping company.'

A shaft of brilliant moonlight penetrated the clouds and illuminated the entire tree. Now she saw the sorry state Tawny Owl was in. 'Oh, what a mess,' she commiserated with him. 'I'm so sorry you fell. I had no idea there was such a trap.'

'Neither had I,' Tawny Owl remarked ruefully. He was partially soothed by her words. 'I may as well admit it – I'm too old for such capers. For the time being you'll have to catch enough food for both of us. I feel as if I couldn't fly at present to save my life.'

'I'll go at once,' Holly said willingly. 'I owe you that much. You stay here and rest.'

Tawny Owl watched her disappear over the gardens. She was absent a long time. Once or twice he tried his wings but each time he nearly overbalanced because his encrusted talons prevented him from gripping the branch properly. When Holly finally did return, carrying three mice in her beak, Tawny Owl could hardly move at all. It was as though his wings were encased. He felt weighed down and almost rigid.

'I don't know what I've done to myself,' he blurted out. He sounded scared. 'I seem to have lost the use of my wings. I think I may never be able to fly again!'

10

The Tainted Stream

Since their meeting in the Hollow the Farthing Wood animals and their dependants had continued to visit the Pond when they needed to. However they were sensible about it and took pains to ensure first that Trey was not in the vicinity. Meanwhile they began seeking out some of the other stags. Fox's message was received with varying responses. Most of the stags were indignant at Trey's presumption.

'Drive me out of the Park? He wouldn't dare go that far,' said one.

'This Reserve is for all the deer, no matter whether one is stronger than another,' said a second.

Some of them were disbelieving. 'How do you know his intentions? He's made no such threat to me,' one questioned.

'Preposterous! The Warden would never allow it. He has to look after the entire herd,' remarked another.

Another saw the impossibility of it straight away. 'How could Trey do it with a fence all around the Park's perimeter?' he demanded.

There were others who were obviously intimidated already by Trey's commanding presence. 'I have no quarrel with him.' 'I'm no contender to be the Great Stag's heir. Trey won't bother with me.'

But all in all the animals succeeded in at least implanting the idea in the male deer's minds that one of their numbers had too low an opinion of his fellows. This naturally rankled and, slowly, a general resentment of Trey's air of superiority began to build up. Fox still hoped that when the time was ripe the haughty stag might find he had assumed too much.

The summer sun shone on the Park and dried out the puddles and pools that had lain so conveniently close to Badger's set since the rainy season earlier in the year. As the stream was still shunned by his friends, Badger realized that before long he too would have to make a trip to the Pond. It would be a laborious journey for the old creature. His sight was now very poor and his legs were stiff and often ached, especially when he tried to be too energetic. But he had to drink like everyone else and one evening he stood just inside his set entrance, sniffing the breezes and vainly attempting to detect a hint of approaching rain.

'It's no use,' he muttered to himself. 'I shall have to make a move. Everything around here's as dry as can be.' And he shuffled off in the direction of the Pond. He hadn't gone far when he halted abruptly. 'This is silly,' he said. 'The stream's much closer. How do we know there's anything wrong with it? I could go and look for myself anyway.' He didn't turn round at once. He was in two minds about it.

'Suppose I should find something wrong there?' he pondered. 'Then it would be even further for me to go across the Park to the Pond. It's a nuisance the stream's the opposite way. Oh dear, now what shall I do?'

In the end his own curiosity as well as comfort decided the issue. He headed for the stream. It was a close muggy evening and Badger was soon tired. He was glad when he could see the stream in the distance because by then he was very thirsty indeed. When he reached the nearest bank he stood and looked at the water for a long time. The stream was low and slow-moving but, apart from that, didn't appear to be any different from usual as far as Badger could make out.

'Of course my eyes aren't the best judges in the world,' he told himself. 'I'll just go down the bank and see if the water smells as it should.' He grunted as he stumbled down to the stream's edge. He sniffed carefully and methodically. His sensitive snout had lost none of its powers. He raised his striped head. He was still uncertain. There was nothing definite and yet. . . .

'I'll just go a little way along to see if anyone else is drinking,' he decided.

It wasn't long before he did indeed hear the sound of an animal drinking. It was a dainty quiet lapping, not at all like the noisy habit of a fox, for instance. He peered ahead but it was too dark for him to see what creature was there. He hurried on. He wanted to talk to any animal who might know something he didn't. But all at once the sounds of drinking ceased.

'Don't go!' Badger called. 'Whoever's there – please wait. I'd like to speak to you.'

There was silence. Badger didn't think the animal had moved off. He heard no noise of its departure. He guessed it was waiting to see him before deciding if it was safe to remain.

'It's only me – old Badger,' he reassured the animal. He shuffled on.

'All right, I'll wait,' the animal called back. It was obviously satisfied it was not in danger.

Badger could tell from the voice it was a rabbit's, but not one he knew well. The rabbit came into view. When it saw Badger it paused on the lip of the bank. Its body was taut, ready to spring away hastily if necessary. Badger came puffing up. 'You – you were drinking?' he enquired.

'Yes.'

'Notice anything strange about the water?'

'No.'

'No funny taste or – or – anything?'

'No.'

'Well that's a relief,' Badger sighed. 'It'll save me a lot of effort anyway.' He headed straight back to the water's edge and bent his head. He took a couple of laps.

'*He's* not around, is he?' the rabbit suddenly asked nervously.

Badger raised his head. 'Who's "he"?'

'The – the deer,' the rabbit answered. 'The massive one with antlers like oak branches.'

Badger was puzzled. 'No–o,' he said slowly. 'There's

no deer around here. Are you referring to the stag called Trey?'

'I don't know his name but – he's mean and aggressive. He drove me off.'

'Off what?' Badger asked.

'Off his territory, he would claim,' the rabbit replied. 'That's why I came here to drink. It's been so dry, hasn't it? I had to come here. I didn't want to. The others said it was a risk, but what was I to do? It's water, at least, even if it is . . . is. . . .' It didn't finish. Its voice died away.

Badger was alarmed. 'Is what?' he gasped.

'I don't know,' the rabbit said. 'There've been stories. Birds dying here and – and – I don't know what else.'

Badger guessed the situation now. 'You were prevented from drinking at the Pond. That's it, isn't it? So you came here?' His questions were urgent.

'Of course. I told you. I wouldn't have come here otherwise.'

'What about the others in your warren? They have to drink, don't they?'

'They were lucky. They got back from the Pond in time. I was the last. He – he was standing there like a sort of sentry as if he'd been waiting for me.' The rabbit coughed.

'What's the matter?' Badger snapped sharply. He was on edge.

'Nothing. I – I'm not sure,' said the rabbit. 'Just a sort of – tickle.'

'A tickle?'

'Yes. My – my throat feels sort of hot.'

'You'd better get back to your burrow,' Badger advised him.

'I will, but now I feel so dry again. I must have another drink.' The rabbit ran towards the stream.

'Don't!' Badger called. He was full of dread. But the rabbit was heedless in its desperation to get to the water. It drank deeply. Now Badger waited for something awful to happen. He was in a turmoil of expectation. The rabbit turned and ran up the bank, seemingly none the worse. It ran straight past Badger as if it had forgotten him entirely. Badger hastened after the animal. He wanted to keep it in sight.

The rabbit, of course, was far fleeter of foot. In no time at all it was lost from sight. Badger forced his aged body into a shambling run. He was desperate to see what would become of the rabbit. His weak eyes probed the darkness. For a while he saw no trace. He didn't even know if he had taken the right direction. But then, all at once, he knew he had. He glimpsed the rabbit ahead. The unfortunate creature had slowed almost to a halt and was staggering about uncertainly as if it had lost its sense of balance. Badger lumbered up, gasping hoarsely.

'What – what. . . .' he wheezed, but he was so short of breath he could manage no more.

The rabbit muttered: 'The burning, the burning . . . I – I'm –' It began to shake uncontrollably. It couldn't keep its feet. It toppled over and lay still. Its eyes stared up into Badger's face. It was dead.

Badger's sides heaved painfully. He stared back at the lifeless eyes in horror. Eventually he got his breathing under control. 'The stream's a killer,' he whispered to himself in the utmost dismay. 'I've drunk from it too. Oh, why was I so foolish? Better to have tired my legs out going to the Pond than this! What shall I do now?'

He tried to recall how much of the water he had drunk but he was in such a state of shock and anxiety he couldn't be sure. He only knew he was still extremely thirsty, as if he hadn't drunk at all. 'The rabbit had a raging thirst, too,' he wailed. He tried to calm himself but it was difficult. 'Pull yourself together. An old animal like me behaving so stupidly! I can't last for ever anyway. I was lucky to come through another winter,' he reasoned. Yet it was hard for him not to feel frightened.

'It may be too late,' he went on, 'but I must try to get to the Pond. If I drink some clean water it might . . . yes, yes, it might help.' He felt better now he had made the decision and he wasted no more time. With a last glance at the poor dead rabbit he trotted away. He could think only of filling himself up with untainted water. All thought of Trey, and why the rabbit had gone to the stream to begin with, had vanished from Badger's mind.

Several times on the way he stopped to regain his breath. He felt very alone and wished heartily for a friendly face to appear. But he saw no-one until he reached the Pond and then it wasn't someone who was friendly at all.

It was growing light by the time he got to the pond-side. He pushed his way through the sedges and reeds and lowered his muzzle thankfully. He began to drink.

There was a sound of pounding hooves. 'Stop!' bellowed a deep voice.

Badger looked up. The stag Trey was galloping round the far side of the Pond towards him.

'You've no right to be here!' thundered Trey. 'This is not your area. I know where you come from.'

Badger was astounded. But his keen thirst overrode every other consideration and couldn't be denied. He bent again to lap.

Trey was infuriated. 'Do you defy me?' he boomed. He lowered his antlers threateningly.

'I'm an old animal. I have to drink where I can,' Badger reasoned.

'There are other places.'

'No. There aren't,' Badger answered. He was beginning to feel unwell. Why wouldn't the stag leave him alone?

'I know your area. The stream is closer for you,' Trey contended.

'The stream is tainted,' Badger growled. His discomfort made him bold.

Trey took in his words. 'What do you mean?' he asked more evenly.

'Didn't the Great Stag die there?' Badger cried irritably.

'He was old – like you,' Trey replied. 'His time had come.'

'A pity for us all,' Badger remarked. He was tired of bandying words with this domineering animal.

Unknown to the two of them a third animal had appeared on the scene and was watching them carefully. It was Plucky the young fox who was homeward bound for his earth. He crept closer without being noticed.

Trey bridled at Badger's remark. He thought he would teach this insolent old creature a lesson. As Badger tried once again to assuage his thirst, Trey cried: 'As you're so determined to have the water, perhaps I can help you reach it!' He directed his antlers at Badger's rump and prepared to butt him into the Pond.

Now Plucky guessed the stag's intention and, regardless of any danger to himself, ran up with fangs bared. As Trey ran forwards the young fox caught one of the deer's hind legs in his teeth and gave it a severe nip just above the ankle. Trey's headlong career towards Badger was obstructed but not altogether prevented. The full force behind his antlers was impaired, luckily for Badger. But the amiable old creature still received a considerable clout and he shot out towards the centre of the Pond. Now Trey pulled up and, as the startled Badger struggled to keep his head above water, the stag turned his attention to his attacker. His leg smarted painfully. He saw the youngster whose impudence was beyond belief.

'This time I'll make you pay!' roared Trey.

Plucky raced round the edge of the Pond with the stag on his tail. The fox feinted and changed direction like a hare, dashing this way and that. Trey's bulk was far less manoeuvrable. He couldn't catch the fox any more than he had Leveret and his anger was at boiling point. Plucky kept an eye on Badger in the water while he zipped this way and that. Badger was swimming gamely and was aiming for the opposite side. He had swum more than halfway across the Pond and the Edible Frogs who inhabited this spot most of the time were urging him on. Badger was so tired he was deaf to all their cries. Now Plucky began calling.

'Come on, Badger! Come over this way. There's a deserted set close by. He can't catch us!'

And Trey couldn't, try as he might. Plucky held him at bay, chasing this way and that and, eventually, the exhausted Badger, his bristly coat pouring water, pulled himself out of the Pond. He wanted only to collapse in a heap in a place of safety. His head was spinning, his throat irritated and his rump throbbed unmercifully but he kept going towards the hole in the ground. It was so close, so close. If only he could get inside it. But now Trey tried to head him off.

Plucky dashed up courageously and, dodging the stag's feet, jumped up to sink his teeth high up in Trey's thigh. Badger made his escape and bolted into the empty set. But even now he couldn't rest. He feared for the young fox. So he turned around in the tunnel and hauled himself back up to the entrance. Plucky was dancing about but now he had risked too much by coming in so close and Trey was aiming blows with his antlers to right and left. It seemed only a matter of time before one would catch him, with severe consequences to the young fox. Plucky's way to the entrance hole was barred by the stag and Badger could see that, despite his own fatigue, he must enter the fray. Trey's back was before Badger and the gallant old creature looked for a way to rescue the youngster whose bravery reminded him so much of his dear friend the Farthing Wood Fox. When the stag stepped back a pace Badger saw his chance and now he bit deeply into the leg that Plucky had already nipped earlier on. As Trey paused, registering this fresh outburst of pain, Plucky instantly made a dive for the hole and in the next second he and Badger were tumbling over each other in the safety of the tunnel.

Plucky scrambled to the nearest chamber inside the set and Badger crawled after him. He was entirely spent. Outside the set Trey bellowed his fury.

When he could muster up sufficient strength to speak, Badger said to Plucky: 'Once it's dark you must fetch the elders – the Farthing Wood Fox and Vixen.' He gasped agonizingly. 'Bring them here. And my other friends too. All you can find.' He gasped again. 'Tell them,' he panted, 'Badger's finished.'

11

The Animals Gather

For the whole of that day Plucky sheltered with Badger in the abandoned set. From time to time he went along the exit tunnel to see if Trey had gone. The stag hung around for a long while, hoping for revenge. In the end he realized he was achieving nothing and left with many threats of 'getting even' and 'teaching you not to try and thwart a royal stag' roared down the entrance hole.

Badger hardly uttered a word all day except in reply to Plucky's enquiries about his comfort. Every limb in Badger's body ached unbearably. His rump was sore from the blow of the stag's antlers. But, worst of all, his throat was hot and dry and he knew his drink at the stream might prove fatal. Indeed he expected to die. Every so often he was racked by a painful wheezing cough which was a constant reminder of the sufferings of the dead rabbit. Badger could think only of his need to survive through the hours of the coming night. It was imperative he give his warning to his friends. He willed himself to hold on.

At long last the late dusk began to descend. Plucky waited a little longer. He was frantic to leave, yet he could not afford the slightest risk. Under cover of darkness he bade farewell to Badger and went up to the entrance hole. He made a thorough check of the Pond's surroundings before actually setting off. There was no scent of deer on the air. He ran round the Pond and, keeping to the shadows as much as possible, made his way to Fox and Vixen's earth as swiftly as his young legs would carry him. There he related to them all that had happened. He knew nothing of the events at the stream.

'We must go to him at once,' Fox said. 'We won't wait for the others. Plucky, I leave it to you to tell them about Badger. Quickly now, explain to me where this set is.'

Plucky gave him the necessary directions.

'Come on, Vixen,' said Fox. 'I hope to goodness we'll be in time.'

The pair of foxes were silent as they picked their way across the Park. They were both deeply worried by Plucky's message. Fox himself, of all creatures, was closest to Badger. Their association and friendship went back such a long way that Fox simply couldn't bear to think what life would be like without him.

Vixen knew as well as if he had told her himself that these thoughts were passing through Fox's mind. Her sympathy for him was intense and, coupled with this, was her own grave concern. For Badger was her friend too. Next to Fox and her own offspring she had more affection for the kind-hearted old animal than any other creature. So it was a sad and sombre pair who arrived at the pond-side.

They were surprised to find Toad there waiting for them. 'I've been to see him,' Toad told them without preamble. 'The frogs told me what had happened when I arrived for a bathe. He really does look as if he's on his last legs.'

Fox and Vixen looked at each other unhappily.

'The set's this way,' Toad prompted and went on ahead, half-crawling and half-hopping until he reached the entrance hole.

'Is – is he badly injured?' Vixen asked with bated breath.

'I don't think so,' Toad answered. 'He's more concerned about something else. He begged me never to swim in the stream. It's the stream that's on his mind more than anything.'

Fox and Vixen hesitated no longer but followed the tunnel down to the chamber where Badger lay in agony.

'Fox! Vixen!' he croaked. 'Thank goodness you've come. I've managed to hang on for you.'

'Oh Badger, my dear, dear friend. You sound terrible,' Fox whispered. 'What's happened to you?'

'I'm done for, Fox,' Badger wheezed. 'It's all up with me. The stream has been poisoned somehow and I've drunk from it. None of you must ever go near it again. You must promise me!' he gasped insistently.

'Of course we promise,' Fox said. 'But how do you know all this?'

Badger told them about the rabbit and how he himself had unsuspectingly lapped the water before he had realized the danger. The foxes and Toad were unable to speak.

'Where are the others?' Badger asked. 'Where's Mole? And Weasel? They must promise too. I must know they're safe.'

'Plucky will find them. He'll find everybody,' Fox reassured him.

Badger relaxed. He was satisfied for the moment. He lapsed into silence but his friends listened to his harsh breathing with mounting alarm.

'Oh Badger, poor Badger,' Vixen wailed. 'Is there nothing we can do for you?'

'Nothing,' he answered. 'Don't fret yourself, dearest Vixen. There's nothing *to* be done. I've no complaints. I feel calm about it now. I've only myself to blame for what must come.'

Toad took Fox aside. 'Look here,' he said urgently, 'we can't just leave him like this. There's the Warden. D'you remember how he helped Badger before when he injured himself? Perhaps he could –'

'This is no injury, Toad,' Fox interrupted quietly. 'It's something much more serious. Even human help could do nothing. We all have to face this some time but – but –' his voice shook noticeably – 'it's difficult to bear, isn't it?'

'Then all we can do is to stay and comfort him,' Toad murmured sadly.

'Yes,' said Fox. 'We won't leave him now.'

Badger was extremely tired and he fell asleep. His wheezing breaths whistled in the dark underground chamber. Fox, Toad and Vixen remained nearby. They sat gloomily and scarcely dared to exchange a word. Later they were joined by a very subdued Weasel.

'Plucky is going to look for Whistler and Adder in the daylight,' he told them. 'Friendly and Charmer are coming but I told them to come unaccompanied. Badger could only cope with his oldest comrades, I think? The younger foxes will have to stay away. There wouldn't be room for them and the old fellow might be overwhelmed.'

'Too difficult a journey for Mossy, I suspect?' asked Fox.

'Yes. But Plucky said he's in a terrible state about this.'

'Mossy and Badger almost shared their homes, didn't they?' Vixen remarked.

'Just like dear old Mole in Farthing Wood,' Toad commented.

'I hope Badger won't start asking for him,' whispered Fox. 'I really don't think I could endure it.'

Daylight came but didn't penetrate the general gloom of the set. However Badger's breathing had eased a little. He awoke to find Friendly and Charmer had swelled the numbers. He made the newcomers swear never to visit the stream.

'Is everyone here now?' he murmured weakly. 'No – I don't smell Mole or Adder.'

'Adder's on his way,' Weasel told him, though he didn't know it for sure. 'It's a long crawl here for him and he'll have to be particularly careful now it's light.'

'Yes, yes,' said Badger. 'There mustn't be any

accidents on my account. That crazed stag has sworn to get even with us.' He was thoughtful. 'Perhaps it would be better for Mole to stay out of harm's way.'

'Thank goodness,' Fox whispered to Vixen. Then he spoke up. 'He's doing just that, Badger. No point in his coming, is there? He never visits the stream any-way.'

'Oh dear,' Badger sighed mournfully. 'I should have liked to see Tawny Owl just once before I –'

He broke off as he heard the sound of another animal arriving. Leveret had raced to the set and tumbled into it almost under the nose of Trey who had recommenced patrolling the area.

'He's got us bottled up here all right,' he announced as he joined the others. 'He's only waiting for one of us to make a false move.'

'He'll have a long wait then,' Friendly remarked grimly. 'He hasn't outwitted us yet.'

The animals listened to Trey's angry snorts outside the entrance hole. The stag stamped up and down, first one way, then another.

'He – he's standing guard over us,' Leveret mur-mured in awe.

They heard his regular hoof-beats. Sometimes Trey called out threateningly although he had no knowledge there was such a large gathering of creatures around Badger.

'This is sheer nonsense,' said Fox. 'Whatever can possess an animal to bear such a grudge?'

'His pride's offended,' Badger said. 'So far we've got the better of him. We've outrun him and out-manoeuvred him. And he's got the scars to prove it.'

'Scars?' Fox asked. 'What scars? I didn't know about this.'

'Plucky and myself left our teeth-marks on him,' Badger said.

'Did you though? My word, Badger, I don't think your days can be over after all. You attacked that huge stag!'

'Yes,' said Badger. 'It's not another animal that's put paid to me, you see, Fox. It's my own stupidity.'

'If Trey's been injured by his encounters with us it does put a different complexion on things,' Fox remarked. 'It's my opinion he'll be determined to redress the balance. He's a vain beast. How belittling for him that he's the dominant deer in the herd yet he's suffered humiliations from creatures far smaller than himself. We'll all have to be doubly cautious.'

It was late in the day when Adder, by subtle and hidden movements, arrived near the Pond. Several times during his journey he had been on the point of giving up. He wasn't known for demonstrations of deep affection or concern. He was, by his very nature, an unemotional animal. But each time he stopped some thought of Badger or some image of him in one of his acts of bravery or kindheartedness compelled the snake to continue. He saw Trey pacing up and down the length of the Pond and it took him an age to get to some cover close enough to the set so that he could get himself into it without trouble when the stag was most distant.

As Adder lay hidden amongst the sedges he saw Whistler fly in and begin a search of the terrain. He was looking for the position of the set where the animals were sheltering, although there was no possibility of his entering it himself. He seemed to Adder to be in a state of excitement. The whistle of his damaged wing sounded rhythmically over the water. Inside the set the animals detected the sound.

'Whistler's agitated,' Fox observed shrewdly. 'His wing's like a second voice. It's evident he can't settle.'

'The stag must still be around,' Friendly suggested.

'I think our heron friend wants to tell us something,' said Weasel.

Adder was thinking the same thing as he watched the great bird's flight. All at once the heron's sharp eyes picked out the snake's familiar patterned coils amongst the waterside vegetation. Taking careful note of Trey's position Whistler descended and, flapping briskly to steady himself, landed close to Adder's little nook.

'What are you doing?' hissed the snake. 'You couldn't make my presence more obvious if you were to pinpoint me with your bill!'

'Sorry,' croaked the heron. 'But I've made an important discovery about the stream. I can't get into Badger's shelter and I thought *you* could tell the others.'

'Tell them what?' Adder rasped crossly. 'The stag's turning this way!'

'It's the humans,' Whistler confided. 'They've poisoned it. They've dumped –' He interrupted himself and took awkwardly to flight as Trey began his approach. 'I'll be back!' he cried hurriedly.

'Irresponsible chump,' Adder muttered as he buried himself deeper inside some dead leaves. The deer was running to investigate.

Whistler was high in the air by this time and Trey

could find nothing on the ground, try as he might. Adder's camouflage was good enough to fool all but those with the keenest sight. Nevertheless he didn't choose to stay put and afford the heron a second chance of blowing his cover. As soon as Trey had wandered away again Adder emerged from his nest of leaves and slithered determinedly towards the set entrance.

Even then, when Whistler saw his movement, he endangered Adder's dash for safety. 'No, wait!' he called to the snake. 'I didn't finish. It's important!' he bawled at him thoughtlessly.

Adder cared nothing for its importance. Deaf to all entreaties he increased his effort and slid into the hole, cursing the heron roundly all the way.

'Bird-brained, bird-brained,' he hissed to himself over and over again until his anger was cooled by the mustiness of the earthen tunnels.

Weasel came to look. 'It's you!' he greeted him. 'Whatever's the fuss about? Badger needs quiet.'

'It's lucky that dolt of a heron can't get in here then,' Adder observed waspishly. 'He's worked himself into a lather about something and did his best to get me skewered on a pair of antlers!'

'Calm yourself,' said Weasel. 'This isn't the time for recriminations.'

Adder realized he had forgotten himself, though he didn't admit it. 'How is he?' he asked, referring to Badger, as he followed Weasel down the tunnel.

'Hanging on.'

'I'm afraid Badger's made himself an example for the rest of us,' Adder lisped. 'His suffering is our warning.'

'That's exactly why he's called us all here. We've all had to swear not to go near the stream. You'll be made to go through the ritual too.'

Badger was the last to hear Adder's voice though he was listening hard for each new arrival. In his old age he had become increasingly deaf but he was relieved when the others told him the snake had at last joined the throng. Adder dutifully went through the motions of promising never to enter the stream.

'I'm glad I've been able to make you the promise,' he said afterwards. 'I wondered if I'd ever talk to you again. Is the – er – pain very acute?'

'No worse and no better,' Badger answered cryptically. 'But I'm so parched, you see. I think I could drink the Pond dry. And I haven't eaten for an age, either.'

The animals began to murmur together questioningly.

'What?' Adder hissed. 'Are you saying you have an appetite?'

'Yes, I suppose I am,' Badger admitted. 'I don't think my stomach has a scrap of food in it.'

Adder's tongue flickered busily. 'Do you mean to tell me,' he demanded indignantly, 'that I've scraped my scales across the breadth of the Park merely to hear you complain that you're hungry?'

'Well, I – I can't help it, Adder,' Badger mumbled. 'It's only natural, isn't it?'

'No, it isn't,' Adder contradicted. 'Not for an animal who is supposed to be dying, and that's what I was told you were. D'you think I would have come all this way otherwise? There's nothing wrong with you. You're an old humbug, Badger!'

'There *was* something wrong with me. There was,' Badger insisted defensively. 'But, the truth is, I do begin to feel better.'

'How much of this so-called killer water did you actually drink?' Adder asked next.

'Um – I don't remember exactly,' said Badger. 'I was interrupted. I'd begun to lap and –'

Now Weasel cut in. 'So you only took a few laps? Then why all this bother?'

'How can you talk like that, Weasel?' Vixen asked. 'Badger saw the rabbit die. What was he to think? And we should be celebrating, not complaining. Poor Badger!'

'Of course, of course,' Weasel said contritely. 'I'm delighted. You know I am. We all are. I didn't mean . . . oh Badger, forgive me. It's such a surprise, that's all, after expecting the worst.'

The animals all began talking at once, congratulating Badger and each other on a false alarm. Adder remained silent. He was certainly pleased Badger wasn't going to die, but he couldn't quite manage to mask his irritation at the unnecessary journey. Then he remembered Whistler. He waited for the hubbub to die down.

'Listen, everybody,' he lisped. 'There's a message about the stream. Whistler has discovered something. He wants to tell us.'

'We can't leave here till dark,' said Toad. 'Will he stay around?'

'I'll go and see if he's waiting,' said Fox. 'It must be nearing dusk.' He went up the exit tunnel and peered out. The light was indeed fading. He saw Trey standing by the pond-side at some distance. He was drinking. Fox pushed his head out and called. 'Whistler! Whistler! Are you there?'

There was no answer. Fox waited. But the heron failed to appear.

'He must be planning to return at dark,' Fox said to himself. He looked again at the stag and his anger began to kindle. 'Whatever's the matter with that creature?' he muttered. 'Will he never give up? What does he intend to do? He can't slaughter us all. I refuse to allow ourselves to be holed up like this for as long as he chooses. We can do better than this! We'll soon test his resolve.' He hurried back to the others.

'Badger, are you sure you'll be all right now?' he asked first.

'Yes. Yes, I think so, Fox. If I could only eat something.'

'That's just it. We're not going to stay here. We've all got to eat. What are we thinking of, letting this deer dictate to us?' He was trying to rouse them.

'Oh-ho, this is more like the Farthing Wood Fox,' Friendly remarked to Charmer, his sister.

'We ought to be able to deal with this customer,' said Fox. 'After what we've been through in the past.'

'That's the spirit,' said Weasel. 'I'm with you, Fox.'

'Me too. Goes without saying,' said Friendly.

'I'll back you up,' said Toad, 'though my contribution may be a bit limited.'

Adder brought him down to earth. 'Contribution to what exactly?'

'I – I'm not sure,' Toad admitted. 'What had you in mind, Fox?'

'Oh, only that we're going to leave this little refuge now. We'll go together. We're going to live our normal lives. If Trey has been injured by some of us he brought it on himself. There's every reason to defend oneself in an awkward situation. He must understand that. So – what are we waiting for?'

'I – I don't feel quite ready for a scrap just yet,' Badger said. 'I've got no strength to rely on.'

'Of course not. We weren't intending you to join in,' said Friendly. 'You must stay here and we'll bring you back something to sustain you for a while.'

'I'm so glad I was able to get you all together,' said Badger. 'What a joy it is to have such friends. Now I know we're all safe. There's only one thing I'm unhappy about: Tawny Owl's absence. He won't know about the dangers of the stream and if he should take it into his head to steal back some time without our knowledge we couldn't warn him about it.'

'No good worrying about him, Badger. He's out of reach,' said Weasel.

'If I know Tawny Owl,' said Charmer, 'the first thing he'd do on his return is to find a comfortable spot for a nap! And we all know his favoured places, don't we?'

'All right,' said Fox. 'Enough of talking. Let's face the foe and see just what that supercilious deer is made of!'

He led the way up the tunnel. Friendly, Vixen and Charmer followed directly behind. Weasel went next with Leveret and Toad and Adder brought up the rear. Outside the set it was now almost dark. The first animal they saw, sitting by the water with the utmost composure, was Plucky.

He leapt up. 'Is Badger –' he began anxiously.

'He's blossoming,' Adder drawled sarcastically. 'He simply loves all this attention.'

Plucky was quickly acquainted with Badger's recovery. He was tremendously relieved. 'What wonderful news,' he said. 'And now I've some for you. I've persuaded Trey to quit.'

'What? How? How could you –' Fox floundered.

'I told him the other stags were rejoicing in his absence,' he answered, 'and that they were becoming extremely friendly with the hinds. I didn't need to say more. You should have seen him gallop. I don't think the dust has settled yet.'

'Well!' exclaimed Vixen.

'*Very* well,' said Friendly. 'Plucky, you're a chip off the old block.'

A Royal Stag

The animals dispersed to follow their own immediate concerns. Chief among these was food. Plucky carried the good news of Badger to Mossy who had been racked by misery ever since he had believed he would never see Badger again. The little mole was so excited he could scarcely wait for the old animal to return to his own home.

'He's got to lie low for a bit,' Plucky told him. 'Get his strength back. Fox and Vixen are collecting food for him.'

Badger lay for a while in the deserted set without moving. The aches in his body were subsiding and the dominant discomfort he felt was still his sore, parched throat. In the end he had no recourse but to stir himself. He lumbered slowly out of the underground chamber and into the tunnel, and from there very, very slowly towards the set entrance. He knew nothing about

Plucky's clever trick on Trey but he was so desperate for water he no longer cared whether the stag was waiting in ambush for him or not. He sniffed at the night air. He could detect no deer odours. Painfully Badger forced his weak, quivering legs over the short stretch of ground to the Pond. He fell on his face in the cool water and gratefully let it wash over him, gulping it down in great draughts. He lay still for a while. It was bliss in the refreshing water. There was no sound nor sight of the stag and Badger was in no hurry to move. What a lucky escape he had had! If he hadn't come across the rabbit he would surely be dead by now. As it was, he had come pretty close to it.

He wondered what Whistler had managed to find out about the stream's danger. Whatever it was, it would be something beyond the scope of mere beasts and birds to rectify. He hauled himself out of the Pond, deliciously wet, and tottered back to his temporary base. Moments later Fox and Vixen returned, carrying roots, tubers and a variety of carrion in their jaws.

'Eat, my friend, eat,' said Fox when he had deposited his load on the hard-trodden earth. 'We want you back with us in our corner of the Park. And your path is clear.' He told him about Trey's abrupt departure.

Badger began eagerly to eat. Fox was amused and approving. 'Badger – the great survivor,' he joked. He and Vixen were supremely happy at their old friend's good fortune.

Badger despatched a succulent root with relish. 'I've had an idea,' he said suddenly as if he had surprised himself. 'There may be a way we can rid ourselves of the stag's threat permanently.'

'We're all ears,' Fox told him interestedly.

'We could make the stream our ally.'

Fox wasn't sure if he understood Badger's suggestion correctly. 'You're not thinking we should persuade Trey to drink from it, are you?' he asked.

'Of course that's what I'm thinking. He's not aware of its danger as far as I know.'

Vixen wouldn't hear of it. 'That's not like you, Badger. It would be an act of betrayal. We've never acted treacherously towards another creature.'

'He's made himself everyone's enemy,' Badger pointed out. 'We had no quarrel with him.'

'That's true,' said Fox. 'But, my dearest Vixen, your heart's in the right place. Trey has no wish to kill any of us; only to dominate the entire Park. So how could we plot his death?'

Badger relented. 'You always were a wise counsellor, Vixen. I bow to your better nature. But I think you're wrong about the stag. After our recent tussles with him I'm sure he'd do anything within his power to avenge himself and it may be some creature will lose its life. I'm not known as a belligerent animal, but if it's a choice between Trey's life and one of my friend's – well, I'd adopt any means to save a friend.'

'It hasn't come to that yet, Badger, thankfully,' Vixen said. 'He's preoccupied with watching the other stags at present. Perhaps we'll have no further brushes with him.'

'I doubt that,' said Badger bluntly. And there the subject was left.

Fox wanted to know more about the stream's mystery and so he sought out Whistler.

'I've been trying to locate some of you,' the heron said petulantly. 'Adder was little help, though I asked him to be. I'm afraid I'm not as stealthy as he and I alarmed him. I wanted you all to know that I've found a clue to the stream's impurity.'

'What is it?' Fox barked. Whistler's long-winded manner could sometimes be infuriating.

'Outside the Park where the stream is joined by a ditch, humans have left their debris. We all have good cause to know how careless humans are about tainting the land. No doubt they're as mindless about water. The rubbish, whatever it is, has contaminated the ditch and the water from the ditch flows into the stream. So it seems very likely to me that –'

'Yes, Whistler,' Fox cut in. 'I understand your drift, and it all sounds very feasible. What made you investigate this?'

'The stream was my chief source of food,' the heron explained. 'Naturally I've wondered why there have been no fish. Now I have to fly a distance to feed. It's very inconvenient. But I think the damage to the stream must be irreparable. It's completely devoid of life.'

Fox pondered the cruel thoughtlessness of humans. 'They poisoned the Great Stag,' he murmured. 'Thanks to them, we have Trey in his place.'

'Countless smaller animals have died there too,' Whistler remarked. 'The entire surroundings have become barren.'

'Even Badger was nearly killed,' Fox growled.

'Wildlife is helpless in these situations,' Whistler said. 'We're at their mercy.'

'I wonder the Warden isn't suspicious, with all these deaths occurring,' Fox mused. 'The carcasses are removed, aren't they?'

'I believe so,' Whistler said. 'The larger ones, certainly.'

'Then he must know something is wrong. *He'll* come to our aid. He cares for us.'

'A heartening notion,' Whistler commented. 'But what of the smaller carrion, such as mice and voles? And songbirds?'

'What do you mean?'

'I don't think the Warden would gather *them* up. They'd be less detectable. So they may be taken by predators such as yourself.'

'I don't hunt or scavenge anywhere in that vicinity,' Fox told him. 'Nor do any of my relatives. But I see what you're driving at. If the little animals are poisoned they in turn may poison those that feed off them?'

'Exactly,' Whistler intoned solemnly. 'So the deaths could become more widespread.'

Fox shuddered. 'All because of one act of carelessness,' he said angrily. 'Will they never learn?'

'Learn?' Whistler echoed. 'You said it yourself, Fox. They don't care.'

The animals became more discerning than ever in their eating habits. The time of the rut was approaching and Trey's main concern continued to be potential rivals amongst the other stags. This allowed the hunting animals a breathing space which enabled them to range across the safer parts of the Reserve without fear of hindrance.

Badger recovered sufficiently during this time to be able to return to his old set. Mossy was so delighted to have him back as neighbour that he made Badger a present of a large heap of the plumpest worms and then they celebrated together.

The animals' enjoyment of complete freedom of movement again was to be short-lived. By September Trey's challenging bellows began to boom through the length and breadth of the Nature Reserve. The Farthing Wood community, like all the other inhabitants, listened and marvelled at their power. And they wondered. They wondered if there would be any answering challenges. They recalled the other stags' responses to their suggestions that Trey wanted to drive them out and most of the animals were not very hopeful.

However, as autumn advanced, there *were* other calls and challenges. Other stags roared because it was in their nature to do so at this time. If a challenge was offered them, they had to take it up. Now Trey came into his own. His calls were defiant, scathing, dismissive of any competitor. His were roars of confidence and supremacy. And, pretty soon, the crash of tangling antlers marked the beginning – and end – of the stags' rivalries. Those bold enough to respond to Trey's taunts became acquainted with his massive strength and force. None fought for long. Even as they locked antlers they were pressed backwards, pushed aside, tumbled, glad to wrench themselves free and be chased far away from the proximity of the hinds. The dominance that Trey had threatened and of which he had long boasted was confirmed. The hinds were his for the taking. He was a royal stag.

The Park fell quiet again. The mists of early autumn rose in the evening and in the still air the Reserve was shrouded secretively. An atmosphere of expectancy pervaded the whole area as if it were on edge, waiting for something to happen. . . .

Trey paced his domain in lordly manner. White Deer Park was his kingdom and the inhabitants his subjects. He really believed all were under his rule and he meant to have none stepping out of line. He hadn't the sense to realize that the birds who nested in the Park were as free of his decrees as the air they flew in. As for the animals of Farthing Wood, they were free in another sense. They had freedom of spirit and no creature, not the Great Cat who had terrorized the Reserve, nor even Man himself, had ever managed to break that. And, as White Deer Park held its breath, it was to be Nature who would demonstrate to all her creatures the real meaning of dominion.

13

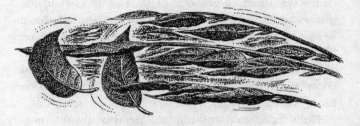

The Hurricane

Tawny Owl was trapped in Farthinghurst. He was unable to stir from the protection of the Great Beech that had, through force of circumstances, become his permanent home. His movements were restricted to an awkward shuffle along the branch he used as a perch. Weighed down by his cement shackles he couldn't fly and it was as much as he dared do to put one foot in front of the other as he waddled miserably along the branch and back again. Even those exercises had to be rationed as he was constantly afraid of toppling over and plunging to the ground. And that really would have been the end of him. But there was one blessing for poor Owl and her name was Holly. The female owl may have led him a bit of a dance at the outset, and indeed had unwittingly brought about his present dreadful situation, but since then she had more than made up for it. All through the remainder of that summer she hunted and caught food for both of them. She never questioned the necessity for this, nor did she complain about the labour of it. Tawny Owl in his misery was not always as appreciative as he might have been. And this was because in his heart of hearts he blamed her for his misfortune.

'I don't feel like a bird any longer,' he would complain to her. 'A bird who can't use his wings is no more than a – a freak!'

Holly tried to comfort him. He was always most miserable when the weather had been dry for a long spell. Since he couldn't leave the tree to drink from a pool or puddle, he had to rely on catching raindrops or dew as it dripped from the leaves of the beech. His thirst was rarely satisfied adequately and he suffered a great deal.

'My body's drying up,' he would moan. 'I should be stuffed and put in a glass box.'

'There will be more rain in the autumn,' Holly would say soothingly. Sometimes she gathered earthworms for him as the moistness of their bodies helped to keep him lubricated.

Tawny Owl had given up all hope of ever seeing White Deer Park again. The ironic situation might have amused a more cheerful creature than he. For he had found his mate, yet was unable to return home with her in triumph. To Owl the bitterest irony of all was that he alone of all the Farthing Wood party who had travelled to the Nature Reserve had actually found a mate from Farthing Wood itself. All the others who had paired long before had found theirs in White Deer Park. Even Fox had found his Vixen during the journey. And Tawny Owl, after the taunts he had received, was beside himself with exasperation that he wasn't able to boast about this to his friends. He longed to triumph over them.

Holly had tried to remove some of the cement from his wings by pecking and tearing at it, but this had proved very painful for him and when he had attempted to do this to his feet the discomfort was so intense he had to give up. Filled with anguish, Tawny Owl had eked out his existence from day to day and week to week with only Holly's companionship to comfort him.

By early autumn one problem at least was alleviated. There were frequent outbursts of heavy rain allowing plenty of water to drip from the tree. There was so much water in fact, that Tawny Owl was often unpleasantly wet. There was nowhere he could take shelter and he yearned for a hollow oak and wings that could carry him there. As time went on he became more and more disconsolate.

'Why bother to bring food for me?' he said to Holly one evening. 'You're only prolonging the agony. I might as well starve and get it over with.'

'That's no way to talk,' she told him. 'Things are bound to get better eventually.'

'Oh yes? And how will they?' he demanded. 'Am I suddenly going to shed these old wings and grow some new ones, like Adder sloughing off his skin?'

Holly had no answer. She simply wished to cheer him up. It was becoming increasingly difficult to do so.

While she was hunting, Tawny Owl used to shuffle up and down the branch that had become his prison.

He ceased to be so careful with the way he placed his feet. 'What difference would it make if I did fall?' he would mutter to himself. 'It would be an end to this misery.' But somehow he never did tumble off and, despite his words, he still preserved deep inside a faint hope that one day, some way, he and Holly would enter White Deer Park together.

The periods of rain increased in length and intensity, exceeding even those during the wet spring. Underneath the beech the ground was sodden. Pools of water appeared in the gardens nearby. The soil couldn't absorb them. The pavements and roads of the Farthinghurst estate streamed with water. Tawny Owl, hunched and shivering, wondered how much more he would have to bear. Holly found the mice were thin on the ground.

'Better try your luck at fishing,' Tawny Owl joked feebly. 'It would be more suitable.'

Holly began to catch more small birds and sometimes insects. She was very adaptable. During the day she sheltered elsewhere from the incessant rain. But at dusk she faithfully returned to Tawny Owl, and during the dark hours she kept him supplied with a share of her catch.

One night, after the two birds had eaten frugally, Holly kept flitting from one branch to another restlessly. She couldn't keep still.

'What's the matter with you?' Tawny Owl asked her testily.

'I feel ill at ease,' she replied.

'Why?'

'I don't know. There's something. . . . Something's going to happen,' she finished.

Her unease eventually communicated itself to Tawny Owl. And there *was* something in the atmosphere. It was charged with a kind of menace. They noticed other birds – starlings and songbirds and suchlike who would normally be safely roosting – stirring from their sites and calling and moving about in a jittery way. The gregarious starlings bunched together as if for reassurance. But it didn't help them to settle and they wheeled about, coming to rest around the roof-tops, then taking off again uncertainly. Sparrows chattered nervously. Small nocturnal mammals scuttled for cover deep inside their bolt-holes. They sensed a great danger was hovering and they instinctively tried to bury themselves away.

It began as a breeze that rustled the vegetation. It was a steady rustling that made the leaves and twigs of the Great Beech quiver. The owls listened. The breeze didn't die away, then return in fits and starts like the usual night breezes to which they were so accustomed. It persisted, as if it were toying with a few ideas before really making its mind up. Then it stiffened, growing rapidly in strength until, with a sudden explosion of force, it roared with a malevolent snarling anger. The beech tree rocked and shuddered. Holly fluttered to a new perch. Tawny Owl could only cling on grimly. But the wind hadn't yet reached its full fury. It expanded into a whirling, devastating violence that battered everything in its path, contemptuous of any resistance. The noise of it was terrifying – a high strident howl that every so often rose to a scream as a gust of unprecedented power tore at the landscape. There had never been anything quite like it before. It was a wind of hurricane force.

The human population of Farthinghurst awoke in darkness as their homes buckled and shuddered. Glass shattered, tiles crashed; fencing, sheds and outhouses were ripped to pieces. Chimneys toppled, roofs caved in and some old or badly constructed buildings collapsed entirely. Everywhere, through the roars and shrieks of the wind, was the sound of destruction. Human ingenuity counted for nothing in the face of this onslaught. Man-made things were as vulnerable as those of Nature's making, rooted in the soil. All life, from the lowliest insect to human beings themselves, were reduced to the same insignificant level before such elemental ferocity. Each could only cower helplessly while it raged.

In the early hours of the morning the storm reached its height. Animal cries of panic were drowned by the deafening roar. Every building rattled and vibrated. Broken materials were bowled along or hurled through the air like pieces of paper. Small plants were flattened. Saplings whip-lashed demonically. Only bushes and shrubs with tightly-knit masses of twigs and leaves could partially withstand the blast. Into their midst burrowed countless terrified birds. In Farthinghurst there were no large trees remaining save the Great Beech. The beech bore the full brunt of the storm's force. Its great branches with their heavy load of foliage bent and groaned and cracked beneath the weight. The roots, loosened by days of rain that had drenched the ground deep down, began to lose their grip. As the tree swayed and shifted, then leant before the assault, Holly abandoned it altogether. She was too frightened to think about anything except her own preservation. She knew the tree was no longer safe. As she left her perch she was caught up in the storm's cruel grasp and tossed like a speck through the air. Her wings spread, she was driven along at tremendous speed until finally she was dashed against a tall hedge. Shaken but otherwise unhurt, she pushed herself into the hedge's denseness like any tiny wren or tit.

Tawny Owl, talons locked as best they could on the splintering branch, waited for the end. The great tree which had withstood scores of lesser storms without damage seemed to heave a last great sigh. Then slowly it gave way. It was as if a giant hand had been plunged into the beech's glossy green hair and was pulling and tugging at it until the whole body underneath lost its balance. The tree toppled, the roots torn from the earth and, with a mighty crash, the last survivor of Farthing Wood prostrated itself on the soil that had nourished it for so long. Tawny Owl was hurled to the ground, yet the force of the wind blew him away from the colossal weight of the beech. As his body struck the soft earth the breath was driven from his lungs. But the brittle cement that had trapped his wings and talons was shivered into pieces. Bruised and gasping for air, it was some time before the bird realized he was free. He lay like a piece of rubbish himself amongst the miscellaneous debris scattered by the hurricane. At last he stirred and instinctively struggled to his feet, flapping his wings as he did so. His shackles had been unloosed. He found he could fly once more. Yet, ironically, flight now would put him into greater peril than before. He scurried for shelter, bumbling into a small conical cypress that grew in a corner of one of the neighbouring gardens.

Towards daylight the hurricane passed, leaving a scene of destruction in its wake. There was damage everywhere and the countryside round about was changed forever.

Thus the last vestige of Farthing Wood was finally obliterated from the map. Now the Wood only lived in the memory of those who had known it.

14

Dependency

Tawny Owl's first thought, as he nestled amid the thick feathery foliage of the cypress, was for his friends in White Deer Park. He wondered how they had fared during the great storm. Now he knew he could fly back to them, he was eager to begin the return journey and this led him to his second thought which was for Holly. He was glad she had left the Great Beech in time, and could only hope she had managed to find safe shelter somewhere. The wind gradually eased and Tawny Owl looked out through the greyish light at a bruised and battered world. The beech lay motionless along the ground like a slaughtered Goliath. Only the dead leaves on its boughs rustled in the strong air currents that were the aftermath of the hurricane. People were already out of doors, surveying the damage to their property and their neighbours'. Tawny Owl decided to quit his refuge.

He flew up and away and began to call for Holly from the wing. Fragments of cement still clung to his plumage and talons but he was oblivious to them. Soon his cries were answered and he saw Holly emerge from her hedge and fly up to meet him. They were both filled with relief to see that the other had survived. Holly began to question Owl about his miraculous return to flight.

'I have the storm to thank for that,' he told her, 'but there's no time to explain now. We mustn't loiter here any longer. We have a journey to make. Follow me.'

Holly willingly tucked herself into his slipstream and they flew away from Farthinghurst and its shocked and dazed human occupants. Tawny Owl led the way back to the countryside, high across the roads and the marsh towards the place where he had conversed with the squirrels. Everywhere there were changes. Everywhere trees were down; others leant at crazy angles against sturdier neighbours; others again had remained upright but with gaping wounds where huge branches had been ripped off by the butchery of the storm. Tawny Owl couldn't recognize the tree where the squirrels had had their home. It may have survived; it may have fallen. It was impossible to tell. He wondered how much White Deer Park would be altered.

The birds continued to fly throughout the early part of the morning. Tawny Owl wanted to press on while there were not too many humans around. Their numbers were increasing all the time as the morning grew lighter. Tawny Owl knew he and Holly would have to hide themselves away before too long. He was able to steer them towards the orchards, despite the changed aspect of the terrain. Many fruit trees had been uprooted or damaged. The two owls sailed overhead. Neither passed a word to the other. Tawny Owl needed to concentrate on navigating their route. He was searching for Rookery Copse. Holly was content to be led for the moment. She had no regrets about leaving Farthinghurst and considered they had both been very fortunate to emerge from the ordeal of the storm without mishap.

The first clue Tawny Owl had that they were near the copse was in the sky itself. Ahead of them in the distance a dark cloud of uncertain shape moved erratically, now in one direction, now another. It didn't take Owl long to realize that the cloud was made up of birds. They were rooks, dispossessed and disorientated by the events of the night. They wheeled about uncertainly, crying their harsh cries of distress and lament. And soon Tawny Owl saw what was left of the copse. At least half the trees in which the rooks had faithfully built their nests season after season were flattened. The old regular outline of the group of tall trees was punctured by great gaps where the storm had wrought its work. The rooks were in turmoil. Their world was turned inside out. Some of them from the living cloud landed briefly on a branch here and there but took off again almost immediately. The others would follow suit and this descending and ascending and wheeling about went on continuously. The rooks were caught up in a mass panic where none of them knew what had happened or what to do. Rookery Copse had become something different and it was something they didn't understand.

Mindful of his reception there on his previous journey Tawny Owl decided to leave the troubled birds to their own devices. Despite his rough treatment by the rooks he felt a tremendous sympathy for them. All over the countryside, he now realized, wild creatures would find their homes destroyed; their territories strange and unfamiliar. Now, more than ever, he longed to reach White Deer Park again. He was afraid of what he would find but he knew he wouldn't be able to rest properly until he saw it with his own eyes. A little further on he flew down and landed in a dead elm which, killed long ago by disease, had with a strange irony withstood the blast of the hurricane when so many healthy trees had succumbed. Holly perched beside him.

Tawny Owl spoke first. 'You may as well discount what I've told you about White Deer Park,' he said, 'because it will probably look quite different now.'

'Yes,' Holly agreed. 'I've been thinking the same thing. Unless the storm missed it?'

'I don't think we can depend on that,' he answered morosely. 'How I wish we could!'

'It'll still be a Nature Reserve, though. Won't it?'

'Oh yes. *That* won't have changed.' Tawny Owl was about to add that his friends would still be there, too, but he choked the words back. How did he know if they would be? He had been away a long time. And the hurricane must have claimed lives wherever it had passed. 'I'm eager to get back just as quickly as we can,' he told Holly instead. 'But it's a long journey and we have to be wary, because there are bound to be many humans about. I think we should look for a place to roost soon; then we can continue when it's dusk.'

'I'm not a bit tired,' Holly informed him. 'We can fly for as long as you like. I leave it to you as the senior.'

'How very diplomatic,' Tawny Owl remarked wryly. 'Well, come on, then.'

The two birds left the bleached skeleton of the elm tree and continued their flight. Tawny Owl was bemused by the tortured features of the scenery. He felt as if he were flying over a new land. He tried to ignore the devastation beneath them. He knew they were on the correct course for the river: he had been able to gauge their direction from the ruined copse. But every so often the cries of wounded or homeless beasts and birds could be heard as the owls travelled past. Sometimes they saw bodies crushed by the force of the storm, lying where they had been hurled. He saw a badger who had been trapped by a fallen tree. And birds – birds everywhere bemoaning their lost nest sites and broken communities. It was then that Tawny Owl feared for his friends and wished fervently that he had never left them. For, whatever horrors they had suffered during the storm, at least he would have been there to share them. That was how it had always been. They had shared all kinds of experiences and hardships and had been able to help each other through their difficulties.

Holly guessed the content of his thoughts every time they became witness to some fresh tragedy. She had no-one to mourn for; she had lived a generally solitary life. Companionship was a new enjoyment for her and the more she appreciated it the more she understood Owl's concern.

'Look out for a likely spot to rest,' Tawny Owl called behind him. He knew the river was not too distant. They were flying over meadows.

Holly scanned the area. There were few trees of any size. But she spied an elder tree which, though not tall, was festooned with a thick cladding of ivy. She thought this might suit their purpose. She flew alongside Tawny Owl. 'Down there,' she indicated. 'There's plenty of cover.'

'Perfect,' he said and they skimmed down together.

There was plenty of space amongst the thick tendrils of the creeper to hide themselves, and they were confident they would be secure. Not that there were any humans in the vicinity. It wasn't a time for people to be out sauntering and taking the air. There were far more important and pressing concerns that day for everyone.

Tawny Owl could hardly wait for dusk. For the first time in many weeks he was looking forward to hunting for himself. Holly had fed him like an invalid for so long he had come to feel quite subservient. He dared not tell her that after their long flight he was well-nigh exhausted. His wing muscles ached abominably. But he told himself he would be more than ready after a good rest. So Holly's next words came as a shock.

'I'll carry on being the provider,' she announced. 'You don't need to pretend any longer to be a bird of prey.' It sounded as if she thought he had become actually incapable of hunting.

'But – but –' he spluttered, so taken aback he couldn't find an adequate response.

'No "buts",' she said firmly. 'I can easily catch

enough for both of us, as you know. You need all the rest you can get. It's a wonder a bird of your age has come through such experiences as you've had at all.'

Tawny Owl was dumbfounded. He couldn't conceive that Holly spoke from kindness and suspected she was insulting him. This was not the sort of association he had wanted to impress his friends with. Why, it was worse than solitude.

'Look here,' he finally managed to say, 'I'm not quite in my dotage yet, you know. I'll admit I'm very tired. It'd be surprising if I weren't. But my hunting days aren't over by any means.'

Holly was amused. 'It's all *right*,' she insisted. 'I understand how you feel. It must have been a humbling episode for you in the beech when you couldn't fly. But it really doesn't matter. I don't mind in the least. I'm younger, fitter, and I can do all that you used to do.'

Used to do! What did she think he was – senile! Oh no. He'd show her. But he smothered his indignation for the present. He decided actions were more telling than words. However, in a short while, both he and Holly were asleep.

Holly awoke first and left the mantle of ivy without disturbing Tawny Owl. It was quite dark and she spread her wings and began to search the meadows. A light shower of rain was falling. Eventually the raindrops which penetrated the ivy aroused Tawny Owl. Realizing his companion was absent he pushed his head out of the creeper and looked for her. At that moment Holly was swooping on a shrew. Tawny Owl saw her pounce and he struggled free of the ivy tendrils and launched himself into flight. He wanted to get clear away before the female owl might return with her kill.

He was surprised to find his flight muscles were painfully stiff. After such a long period of disuse, he had overtaxed them on the first lap of the journey from Farthinghurst. But he bore the aches and soreness with determination. He had to make it clear to Holly at the outset that he could resume catching his own food. The trouble was, his whole body felt incredibly tired and feeble. It was as much as he could do to flap his wings occasionally, merely to keep airborne. So how was he to hunt? He had no speed now and no agility to rely on. Even if he saw some likely prey he doubted if he could direct his exhausted body with sufficient accuracy to make a kill.

'This is absurd,' he spluttered, angry with his physical shortcomings. 'Am I to remain dependent on another? Unthinkable, unthinkable. . . .'

He had to try. Fortunately his eyesight had lost none of its sharpness. He flew over some fields well away from where he had seen Holly pounce. There was no dearth of small creatures running on their habitual paths through the grass-stems. He looked hard for an animal that might be a little slower, a little older, a little more accessible. The diminutive creatures scurried about busily, pausing occasionally to sit on their hind legs to nibble at a tasty morsel or to look and listen for danger. Tawny Owl flew up and down, unable to decide on his target. His wing-beats became more and more laboured and gradually decreased in frequency. His body dropped steadily nearer ground level. And the nearer to the ground he became the more detectable

was his presence to the voles, shrews or wood mice he
was hoping to catch. He soon realized that, unless he
selected his quarry quickly, he would lose all opportunity of a capture. Most of the animals were running
for the shelter of their tunnels. He did see one, however,
who was very absorbed with some particularly appetiz-
ing seeds. Tawny Owl lowered his talons and plunged
towards it. The wood mouse seemed unaware of his
approach. Tawny Owl struck it, grasped it in his beak
and prepared to take off again. The mouse was dead.
He had made his kill and he was filled with a mixture of
pride and relief. But now he found his wing muscles
were too stiff for him to achieve lift-off. He needed to
beat his wings quickly to get airborne, using what air
currents were available to do the rest. But the muscles
were so tired and sore that he could only manage a
couple of quick beats and these were no use at all.
Tawny Owl realized he couldn't get off the ground.

He dropped the mouse. 'Now I really am stuck,' he
murmured to himself. 'I can't even get back to the
roost.' He began fatalistically to tear at the mouse
carcass. At least he could eat where he was. Then all at
once he stopped. He knew Holly would eventually
come looking for him. He would need a longer rest
before he could fly again. And it was important to him
that Holly should see that, although he had over-
stretched himself, he had not entirely wasted his efforts.
So he left the rest of his kill untouched as a sort of
trophy to display to her.

Holly was a long time making her appearance and
Tawny Owl had grown horribly hungry in the meantime. So when he finally saw her gliding above he called

to her in all humility, desperate to break his fast: 'Here!
Here I am!'

Holly's scolding began before she reached the
ground. 'What did I say to you, you silly old bird? I've
been searching for you for ages. I've caught enough
mice to feed a brood, let alone just the two of us.' She
landed and noticed Owl's catch. 'And is that all you
exhausted yourself for? Some other predator's leavings? Now what is to happen? Are you going to stay
here in the open in broad daylight?'

'I caught this, I caught it myself,' Tawny Owl
protested feebly. But it was no use. Holly wasn't
listening.

'I'll go back and fetch some better food for you,' she
told him. 'You'd better eat heartily and build up some
strength. You'll need to exercise those wings before
much longer or I don't know what might happen to
you. And in future,' she nagged him, 'you want to pay
more attention to what I say. You've made a real fool of
yourself – and at your age too! I shall have to keep
watch over you now, just as if you were a helpless
chick.'

She flew away, back to the elder tree, to fetch the
food. She didn't wait for a reply. Tawny Owl groaned.
By trying to assert himself he had ended up becoming
more dependent than ever.

15

No Contest

In White Deer Park, in the last few days before the hurricane reached it, Trey had followed up his triumph by establishing his rule over the whole herd. The other males largely kept their distance but the dominant stag couldn't be in all places at all times and so they were able on occasion to rejoin the hinds. The females were quite content with the situation. When Trey was around, which he generally was, each seemed happy enough to be part of his harem. He was the finest of the stags by far and they recognized his superiority.

The other animals often saw him leading the herd to drink at the Pond. The hinds grouped around its fringes and drank together whilst Trey kept watch for any possible interference. At these times it was not advisable for any creature of the Park to approach too closely. Trey would exercise his self-appointed authority over the Nature Reserve by chasing it away.

He was very jealous of his herd's rights to have exclusive and uninterrupted use of the water. The other inhabitants wondered how much further he would attempt to rule their lives when his present absorption with the hinds was over. He had given them plenty of indications and they tired of seeing him stepping regally along the boundaries of the Park, his head with its heavy burden of antlers held high, and his haughty glance sweeping over the length and breadth of the Reserve.

'It seems his vanity knows no limits,' Fox remarked when the animals were gathered one evening. 'But his legs bear the toothmarks of Plucky and Badger. He's not unassailable.'

'Let sleeping dogs lie,' Vixen counselled. 'He doesn't impose himself on us at present.'

'We've always been free to visit the Pond whenever we needed,' Fox replied. 'All of us. These days, Toad's the only one who's allowed free rein because he's small enough to be overlooked.'

'If only Trey would go and drink from the stream,' Weasel growled, 'it would solve all our problems.'

'It's hardly likely,' said Friendly, 'when every other creature in the Reserve avoids it.'

Adder was bored with this continuous topic of water, perhaps because as a reptile he didn't understand the mammals' preoccupation with the need to drink. 'There's plenty of rainwater lying around now,' he hissed. 'Enough for all the animals in the Park to make use of. Why this constant obsession with the Pond?'

'It's symbolic,' Weasel told him.

'Symbolic of what? Only of unending chatter as far as I can see,' the snake contended.

'It's symbolic,' Weasel intoned slowly, 'of the way our freedom to roam has been blighted by this stag.'

'Oh – oh. Round and round we go,' Adder rasped and coiled himself up as he spoke, so that the others weren't sure if he was being sarcastic or commenting on his own activity.

Weasel, however, was goaded. 'He's right, you know,' he said. 'I can remember days not so very long ago when we did more than just talk.'

'Yes,' said Fox. 'We were young and vigorous then.'

Weasel drew himself up. 'We're still the Animals of Farthing Wood,' he said proudly. 'We've got the better of many a foe in our time. And you said yourself Trey isn't unassailable.'

Fox was interested. 'What do you propose, Weasel?'

'I propose,' he answered, 'that we stand up for ourselves, just like Plucky and poor old Badger.'

'We don't want to meddle with Trey,' Vixen cautioned. 'He's a youthful beast and a strong one and all our wisdom and guile may count for nothing against that.'

'I'm not advocating meddling with him,' Weasel assured her. 'I don't want anything to do with him, personally. But if he continues to meddle with our liberty within the Reserve then, as I say, I think we should stand up for ourselves.'

'Bravo, Weasel. Well said,' Friendly commented. 'Father, why don't you lead our party down to the Pond to drink, just as the stag does with his herd?'

'That's provocation,' said Charmer.

'That's right,' agreed Friendly happily. 'Well, Father?'

'All right,' said Fox. 'It's worth a try. We'll browbeat him. He can't intimidate a whole group of us. He'll have to concede. And, once he's done so, perhaps we shall be allowed to carry on our lives without this constant fear of hindrance.' There was the old authority and determination in his voice.

'We can't travel around in a big group all the time,' Leveret pointed out. 'Supposing he tries to pick us off one by one?'

'We've no reason to fear that,' Fox encouraged him. 'He's shown no sign of it so far. I don't think he's vindictive enough.'

'Nor sufficiently clever,' Weasel added.

'Well, no time like the present,' Fox said confidently. 'I feel two seasons younger already. Who's coming?'

There was a general chorus of support.

'Good,' Fox said. 'Only Badger must stay behind. And Mossy can keep him company.' He turned to the mole. 'Will you make certain he remains in his set?'

Mossy assured him he would.

'Apart from you, then, it's the whole party?' Fox summed up.

'Except for Tawny Owl,' Whistler reminded him.

'I begin to believe we shall never see old Owl again,' Fox said sorrowfully. 'I'm afraid something must have happened to him.'

The younger foxes looked uncomfortable as they always did when Tawny Owl was mentioned.

Fox noted their discomfort and relieved them of it. 'Follow me, then, all of you,' he cried and, quitting the Hollow, set off in the direction of the Pond.

Beside himself and Vixen, only Weasel, Whistler and Leveret were also of the old Farthing Wood contingent. Toad was already at the Pond, Tawny Owl was absent, Badger too feeble, while Adder showed no sign of wishing to uncoil himself. So it was just as well there was a good number of Fox's and Vixen's descendants to bolster the throng: Friendly and Charmer, Pace, Rusty, Whisper and Plucky. Mossy hurried to Badger's set to acquaint him with the animals' move. His short legs were not any swifter overland than his father, Mole's, had been. So an appreciable period had elapsed before he dug himself into the familiar darkness of his labyrinth of tunnels that connected with Badger's home. The old animal took the news badly. He was hurt.

'So they don't think I can contribute anything any more?' he mumbled. 'How could Fox be so unkind?'

'No, no, he meant to be quite the opposite,' Mossy asserted. 'He wants to protect you, I'm sure.'

'Protect me? Nobody needs to protect me,' Badger declared. 'I can look after myself.' He began to lumber up the tunnel.

'Where are you going?' cried Mossy in alarm. 'Fox is relying on me to –'

'To keep me out of it? Oh no. That'll be the day,' Badger growled. 'Where the Farthing Wood animals go, *I* go.' He was quite obstinate. He turned his back on Mossy and headed for the exit. Mossy was powerless to stop him.

'Oh dear,' said the mole. 'I've done this all wrong. Whatever will Fox think of me if Badger's hurt?'

But Badger had no intention of getting hurt. He'd already survived one brush with the royal stag, as well as a near poisoning and he didn't think Providence was against him. As he passed the Hollow he saw Adder enjoying his solitude.

'What are you doing here at such a time?' he demanded.

'Being more sensible than you, by the look of it,' the snake answered, quite unruffled.

'Come on, Adder. We're all together in this.'

'Oh no, Badger. Quite the reverse. We're *not*.'

'Have you forgotten the Oath?'

'No, of course not. But whatever happens at the Pond would have happened anyway long before I could have got there.'

Badger saw the sense of this and realized the same could apply to himself. 'All right,' he said. 'Well, I'll see you later.'

'I certainly hope so,' Adder replied. 'But if you must go, go carefully, Badger. There's something in the air tonight.'

Badger's senses, blunted by age, had not detected anything unusual, besides which his thoughts were thoroughly absorbed with the affront dealt him by his friends. He stumbled along on the trail of the other animals, determined to play his part in the Pond scenario.

The night was well on when the others brought themselves within sight of the expanse of water. As if Fate had ordained it, the first thing they noticed was that the Pond was ringed by the ghostly white blur of deer jostling for positions to drink. Fox's eyes searched for Trey's figure. And there he was, a short distance from his minions, keeping watch over the area. Fox saw the stag's head turning this way and that as he craned his long muscular neck for intruders.

'He's there all right,' he remarked needlessly, for all of them had seen Trey.

The animals bunched together. Whistler landed in their midst. 'What – what do we do now?' Leveret whispered nervously.

'We go forward, of course,' Weasel snapped. 'To drink.'

'Yes, but we won't go blundering straight in,' Fox qualified his answer. 'We've got to be clever about it. The most important thing is that we stay in a tight group.'

'There's room at the far end of the Pond for us all,' Whistler pointed out. 'Well away from where the stag's taken up his station.'

'No, Whistler, that's just what we don't want,' Fox told him. 'It would be too blatant and would only stimulate Trey into immediate action. He'd come charging at us at once, assuming we were out to challenge his authority.'

'But we are – aren't we, Grandfather?' Pace asked.

'There are ways, Pace, of doing these things,' Fox told him patiently. 'An animal of Trey's size galloping at full-tilt would scatter us irretrievably. He'd have won his argument before we'd even begun. No, we're going to, quite literally, fox him.'

The animals enjoyed the pun.

'How do we do that?' Whisper asked.

'By doing what he'll be least expecting,' Fox replied.

'We're going to march right up to him and confront him. He won't be quite sure how to take us.'

'Lead on then, Fox,' said Weasel. 'If anybody can pull this off, you can.'

The animals trod quietly but deliberately forwards, heading directly for the imposing figure of the royal stag. In the darkness it was a while before Trey picked them out. He began to toss his head in a threatening manner. But the collection of animals kept on coming. From the edge of the Pond, amongst some rushes, Toad watched their progress. 'It looks like a deputation,' he marvelled to himself.

'What's this?' Trey bellowed to the approaching group.

Fox waited until they were near enough for him to answer without being required to raise his voice. 'It's a drinking party,' he replied quietly.

Trey's eyes roved over the animals appraisingly. He wasn't sure why they had gathered together but he didn't see anything to test his strength. 'Where are you heading?' he enquired, though he knew the answer.

'To the water,' Fox said.

'There are many suitable puddles all around you,' Trey told them.

'Ah, but they're not suitable for the deer herd, it seems,' Fox said coolly.

'Of course not. The Pond's our source of water.'

'Well then, it shall be ours too,' Fox stated. 'There's plenty of room for each of us and we shan't disturb the hinds. Come on, everyone.'

The band of animals followed Fox and Vixen without a word. They passed Trey and went on towards their destination. For some moments the stag stood stock still. The presumption of the motley group took his breath away.

As they reached the Pond Fox whispered: 'Get in amongst the hinds.'

The animals did as they were bid and pushed themselves between the bulky bodies of the deer as they drank. Some of them got underneath the long legs of the females and in that manner threaded their way through to the water. By this time Trey had identified Plucky, the young fox who had dared to intervene when he had been teaching the old badger a lesson. The sight of this particular animal boldly defying his presence and actually mingling with his hinds galvanized the stag into action. He dashed across the short distance to the Pond, intent on proving his mastery once and for all. But all the animals in Fox's band had become so intertwined with the female deer that Trey was unable to attack. He snorted furiously and galloped up and down looking for an opening.

The hinds had made no objection at all to the smaller animals' presence at the waterside. They were quite used to the existence of foxes and other creatures in the Park. They had always been around and they had no fear of them. Indeed Fox and Vixen, Badger and Tawny Owl were well-known to them and held in high esteem. Trey was unique amongst all the deer in his arrogant attitude and the antipathy he aroused in the other inhabitants of the Reserve. So, while he sought angrily for one of the Farthing Wood band who might have exposed himself to attack, the female deer were welcoming their company at the pondside and docilely engaging them in conversation.

Trey's exasperation was overwhelming. Toad watched his antics with the greatest enjoyment. 'Trust old Fox,' he chortled to himself. 'He's left the stag helpless.'

The animals were free to drink for as long as they chose. Yet many of them were not drinking at all. Their trek to the Pond to confront Trey had been a gesture of independence and the fact was that they hadn't really needed the Pond's water to quench their thirst. Led by Fox, they had been out to demonstrate that they meant to go on using it when the need *would* arise. When the stag realized that they were not drinking, his anger bubbled over. Ironically, the very thing he had been trying to prevent now incensed him the most. He knew their intention had merely been to best him. He roared at his females who were displaying every token of friendship to the other beasts.

'Cease your prattling,' Trey boomed, 'and step away!' He wanted to get at Fox himself now. He knew all about his legendary cunning and he couldn't allow Fox to make a fool of him in front of his harem. The stag was simply seething with rage. Flecks of foam flew from his lips.

The hinds turned to look. Trey pranced about, unable to keep still. Some of the other stags who also used the Pond were hovering not so far off, relishing their conqueror's discomfiture. The females were in no hurry to move. Nothing would have persuaded them to put Fox and Vixen in danger.

'Step away, I say!' Trey roared. 'Or you'll rue the

consequences!' His threats were idle. He couldn't harm his own herd.

A wind blew across the Park, a wind of ill-omen. All the animals – the hinds, the other stags, the Farthing Wood community and its younger relatives – were aware of it. They paused from their activities, raising their heads to look for its meaning. The foxes snuffled the air. Whistler flew over the Pond croaking a warning and birds clustered in the sky in nervous knots. Only Trey, obsessed as ever by his own importance, failed to notice. But his bellows and ranting were ignored.

'We need to find shelter,' said Vixen. 'There's a storm brewing.' Even as she spoke the wind began to moan in the nearest tree tops and send wide ripples chasing each other across the surface of the Pond.

Fox quickly began to round up his group, heedless of the fact that they had now to leave the protection of the clustered female deer. There was a greater danger to pay attention to. The hinds milled around uncertainly.

'Remember the place where Badger thought he was dying?' Fox asked his friends. 'We must go there now. There's no time to get back to our own homes.'

Plucky knew the way to the deserted set better than anyone. It was he who had first discovered it. He trotted off, calling over his shoulder. 'It's in this direction.'

Trey saw his opportunity. 'You've taken one chance too many this time,' he said savagely and began to charge at once, his great antlers lowered.

'Plucky! Plucky! Take care!' Vixen cried and she was only just in time.

The young fox sidestepped the stag's impetuous rush

which carried the foolish animal some distance past him, towards the rest of the group.

Fox was scornful. 'The mighty stag!' he scoffed. 'You call yourself the overlord of the Reserve. Yet you don't seem to have any regard for the danger your own herd is in.'

Now the wind was beginning to howl and strong gusts whipped at the sedges and rushes by the Pond. Trey's anger was cooled, despite himself, by the jittery behaviour of the hinds. They sensed the storm and were fretful, lacking direction.

Fox turned his back and led the animals after Plucky. One by one they entered the set, gaining comfort from each other's company. Whistler joined Toad amongst the rushes.

'No contest,' Toad remarked. 'The Pond's ours again.'

They watched Trey gathering the hinds. Presently the herd moved away from the water's edge.

'They'd be wise to stay in the open,' Whistler commented. 'I hope he has the sense not to lead them under the trees.'

The other stags moved away as Trey approached. The strength of the wind increased in power with every passing minute. In a patch of woodland, not too far distant, Badger urged his ancient limbs to greater efforts. He had travelled too far from his own set to be able to return in safety. He could think only of the alternative shelter where, unknown to him, his friends were already assembled. He was between the two and he knew he had put himself in the greatest peril.

16

Storm Over the Park

In the teeth of the wind the deer herd stood on the open grassland. The other stags wandered ever closer, desiring the reassurance brought by a mass of animals. Trey, however, would only allow them within a certain radius of the hinds. If they overstepped this invisible boundary he corrected them. Some of the males lay down. The vicious wind grabbed at their heavy antlers, threatening to pull them over. The females milled about uncertainly. Trey planted his feet farther apart as he battled to withstand the full force of the wind.

The hurricane quickly reached a crescendo. It became impossible for any of the deer to stand against it. The hinds lay down and gritted their teeth, sheltering their youngsters as best they could. Even Trey succumbed and now all thought of rivalries and possession was forgotten in the maelstrom of air that whirled across the Park. The herd, including the other males, instinctively bunched into a tight-knit group. They listened to the crack! crack! of shattering branches from distant trees. There was a creaking, tearing, ripping cacophony, punctuated by crashes as the root systems of mature specimens in the patches of woodland were loosened from their moorings in the saturated soil and their trunks and branches hurled earthwards. One after another was destroyed. Above the boom of the trees smiting the earth like blows from a steam hammer, the screaming, shrieking wind was the dominant sound. It seemed to laugh and mock at the havoc it caused. The terrified wildlife population of the Nature Reserve cowered in their tunnels and holes or took shelter where they could. Some of them left the Park altogether for the open downland as portions of the boundary fence were torn down, leaving escape routes to the world beyond for those who were driven to take them.

In the abandoned set the community of Farthing Wood animals huddled together, almost too frightened to speak. Every tunnel, every chamber of the underground system was occupied. Fox managed to voice his thoughts to Vixen. 'I'm so thankful that Badger is safe inside his own set.'

As he said it, in that other part of the Park, Mossy dug deeper into the ground while the tempest raged and roared. He had waited for Badger's return when the wind first sprang up, thinking to return would be the old creature's first reaction in the storm. But, as time went on and the storm increased in intensity with no sign of Badger, Mossy began to fear the worst. How he rued his own action in Badger's departure. For, innocent though it was, if he hadn't brought the message from Fox, Badger would have known nothing of the animals' expedition to the Pond and would have been quite happy staying put. So Mossy trembled for Badger so exposed to the power of the elements and longed for a miracle to preserve him. The little mole buried himself deeper and deeper to escape the terrifying noise. As he paused from his efforts, suddenly the whole labyrinth of tunnels and passages shook under the most almighty blow which reverberated underground like an earthquake. Mossy thought the world had fallen in on top of him and indeed, in some respects, his own subterranean world had done so. One of the larger trees in the wooded area where Badger had constructed his home had fallen directly on the set and smashed through the system of passages into the heart of his living quarters. Thus unwittingly Badger had saved himself by his determination to defy Fox's advice.

Yet now, with every faltering, stumbling step he took across the Park, Badger was still risking death. All around him heavy branches, snapped by the wind, were falling to the ground with their heavy loads of twigs and leaves. As he scuttled free from one dangerous spot another bough would break and bar his way. When the trees themselves began to fall he knew he must attempt to get into the open. But his progress was constantly impeded by the huge obstacles which littered every portion of the woodland.

'It looks as if I escaped being poisoned only to be flattened by an oak,' he muttered grimly. 'If that's to be my fate I wish I'd died earlier because now I'll never know if the others survive.'

Somehow he struggled on. The horrific howl of the storm accompanied him every step of the way. Badger pulled himself over or under branches, making a circuit of the larger uprooted trees. Some of these had not been torn entirely free from the soil and still quivered as if in their death throes. At last he saw light ahead at the edge of the woodland. It was so dark under the trees that even a slight lessening of the gloom was markedly noticeable. Clouds raced at breakneck speed across the sky, obliterating the moon and stars. But as Badger – panting, exhausted, terrified – pulled himself over the last hurdle of a mass of flattened vegetation, the hurricane strength of the wind was dropping. Badger forced himself on, putting sufficient distance between himself and the horrible sound of crashing trees. Eventually he could go no further. His shaky legs gave way beneath him and he lay, quite helpless, with the storm roaring overhead. The worst of it, however, was past.

When Trey became aware that the storm's force was slackening he scrambled to his feet to survey the herd. A few metres from where the deer were gathered was a crumbled piece of fencing which had once marked the limit of the Nature Reserve. Next to it a hefty Scots Pine, not quite ripped from the earth, leant at a crazy angle and swayed threateningly with every gust of air. Trey saw the wide gap in the boundary fence and he saw the males of the White Deer herd dotted amongst his hinds. He tossed his great head, almost in defiance at the storm's diminishing power. He was once again the royal stag, jealous of interference. The other males stirred as they saw him towering over the herd. Some of them remembered the tales of how Trey had sworn to drive them from the Park. One by one they stood up, uncertain of their next move. They were not long in noticing a ready-made exit close at hand.

Trey now decided to rid himself of their competition for good. He began to see a way of doing it, thereby fulfilling Fox's prediction, though without realizing it himself. It was growing light. The wind still buffeted the males' antlers, making it hard for them to keep their balance.

'Begone,' Trey ordered the stags. 'The danger is over. Move away from my hinds, I say.'

The males extricated themselves from the herd and wandered off a little way. Trey wasn't satisfied. They hadn't moved far enough. Something about the way the other stags still seemed to be hovering in hope near his females aroused his anger once more.

'*That's* the way, over there, through that gap!' he ordered them.

When they looked at the broken fence and back at Trey in disbelief he began to hustle them.

'I want no rivals near, do you hear? Go now of your own volition or be driven out!' And, to hasten their departure, he cantered towards them with lowered antlers.

Some of the inferior stags took him at his word and actually ran through the gap out of the Park. The hinds watched in amazement. The stouter males saw no reason why they should be forced from their home. But Trey meant to do just that. As they hesitated he singled

one out and charged at him. The animal put up no
resistance. In a moment he had joined those who had
already left. The remainder were not so easily cowed.
They realized that if they didn't make a stand now Trey
would have the Park to himself indefinitely. As he ran
at them they ducked and weaved and sidestepped in
any direction but the one in which he intended they
should go. His temper flared. He managed to connect
with one stag, butting him and bowling him over. The
deer leapt up and ran for the opening. Trey scented
victory. He chose another target, a particularly sturdy
animal, and gave chase. The two stags went round and
round, this way and that. The others looked on in
suspense. Trey drove the other male close to the
leaning pine. The stag stumbled over the broken
fencing, was momentarily overbalanced, and a gust of
wind did the rest. He went sprawling. As he fell he
smashed against the pine tree which began to rock
ominously. Trey, carried forward by the impetus of his
charge, was unable to pull up. As the huge tree teetered
Trey was underneath it. Even as he turned to avoid it
the pine lost its tenuous grip on the soil and fell. It fell
directly on to the royal stag, pinning him down beneath
its weight. The mighty overlord of White Deer Park lay
motionless. The other stag regained its feet. Then the
herd mingled around Trey, looking in horror and awe
at his stricken body. The males outside the Park
returned to gaze at the sight. Trey looked at them
helplessly through glassy eyes. His tongue protruded
from his muzzle. Blood flowed from his open mouth
and collected in a pool under his head.

Dawn broke over the shattered Nature Reserve.

Many trees had fallen. Many lives had been lost. In the Hollow, Adder uncoiled himself and slid away. During the passing of the storm he had not stirred a fraction.

17

Homeless

It was a while before the animals were sure it was safe to leave the shelter of the abandoned set. They had listened to the moan of the wind for so long that the quietness now seemed unreal and they expected the storm to return at any moment. Eventually, when it grew light, Friendly went to the end of the exit tunnel and looked out. Everywhere there was evidence of the path of the storm. Around the Pond the rushes and sedges were flattened as if by some mighty haymaker. At one end a birch tree had fallen into the water, its branches and leaves trailing under the surface. Some of the Edible Frogs were sitting on its trunk. Friendly wondered how many more were squashed underneath. As he looked further afield he could see a wooded area thinned out by the hurricane's savagery. He hurried back to the others.

'It's – it's changed,' he whispered. 'Everything's changed.'

Now all the animals wanted to look. They left the abandoned set and sat in a group around the entrance hole, not quite believing what they saw. The older animals were reminded of their past.

'It's just like Farthing Wood when the bulldozers came,' Fox said sorrowfully.

Weasel tried to raise their spirits. 'But there are many trees still standing or – or – leaning. . . .'

Fox recognized a new danger here. 'We must avoid the wooded areas as much as we can now. Listen! I can hear them creaking.'

Leveret, whose home was in the open grassland, said: 'What about your homes under the trees?' Most of the foxes' earths were amongst the woodland.

'We may have to make new ones,' Vixen answered him. She shook her coat. 'Let's go and see if Toad's all right.'

The animals went to the Pond's edge, calling his name. Toad came crawling eagerly from his rushy bower.

'What a night,' he croaked. 'I thought it would never end. Whistler kept me company. But he's gone now to examine his nest. Fox,' he enthused, 'it's marvellous to see you all safe. I watched you with the stag. How cool you were!'

'Hm. No sign of the deer,' Fox answered. 'I wonder how they fared?'

'The main thing is, *we've* all come through,' Toad said happily. 'But where's Badger?'

'No need to worry about him. He's safe in his own set,' said Friendly.

The animals realized that their priority now was to see how their own homes had suffered.

'Remember, everyone,' said Fox, 'the trees! Tread carefully and avoid creakers. Good luck.'

They left Toad by the water and went their own ways. It was Fox and Vixen who found Badger. The old animal had rallied with the daylight and was creeping about, not sure whether to continue on to the Pond or retrace his steps. The sight of the pair of foxes put new heart into him. He was eager to know whether they had encountered Trey, but first he had to explain to his astounded friends what he was doing there.

'Foolish but loyal creature,' Fox commented warmly. 'And there we were, all of us, congratulating ourselves you were out of harm's way.'

'I did take a bit of a risk,' said Badger. 'Mole tried to prevent me, but I thought you might need me. Did Trey make an appearance?'

'Oh yes, he was there. But we soon dealt with him.' Fox described their tactics. 'I don't think he'll be bothering us so much from now on.' He didn't know how right he was.

'Are you heading homeward?' Badger asked.

'Yes.'

'Will you walk with me? It may take you a little longer because we have to avoid that stretch of woodland – it's full of debris – and, well, I may be rather slow.'

'Of course we'll go with you,' Vixen answered. 'What an unnecessary question. We'll see you to your set.'

'No need to come all the way,' Badger said, keen to

retain some semblance of independence. 'Just as far as your own earth.'

They set off. Badger was indeed slow but the foxes were patient and made no attempt to hurry him. As they progressed they constantly saw new areas of destruction. They discussed the changed aspect of the Park. At one point they spied the Warden in the distance doing his own round of damage inspection. The sight of the man always inspired confidence amongst the animals.

'He'll make it all right again,' Badger murmured trustfully.

'It'll never be quite the same,' Fox contended. 'Remember Farthing Wood. When trees are down. . . .' He left the rest unsaid.

'It's still the Park,' Vixen commented. 'The animals' Park. No human dwellings. We'll get used to the changes.'

As they travelled Whistler was flying to meet them. He had seen Trey's body from the air and so, for the second time in a season, the heron was the first to bring news of the fall of a dominant stag. He scoured the Reserve for a sight of Fox. Presently the three animals heard the well-loved whistle of the bird's punctured wing. With a few mighty flaps Whistler came to rest on the ground a metre or two ahead of them.

'Astonishing news,' he greeted them. 'Our tormentor is a victim of the storm. He's lying by the perimeter fence, crushed under a tree.'

'Trey?'

'None other.'

'Is he dead?'

'Not dead, but utterly helpless.'

Fox and Vixen exchanged glances. They were stunned. Yet they had mixed feelings about the news. Badger, however, had a look of satisfaction.

'The stag has made his last patrol of the Park,' he remarked. 'So that's one of our troubles removed.'

Fox looked doubtful. 'Where is the rest of the herd?' he asked Whistler.

'Milling around the fallen leader,' the heron replied. 'They seem to be in some sort of confusion.'

'Well, it's no concern of ours,' said Badger. 'We have other matters to think about. We don't even know if our homes have survived.'

'Whistler, forgive us,' said Vixen. 'Your news drove every other thought out of our heads. Did your nest survive?'

'No. It's wrecked,' he replied. 'But nests are easy to replace. Not so the trees that supported them.' He left them then to give the news to others of the community.

'Many homes must have been destroyed,' said Badger. 'The birds and squirrels will have fared worst.'

'I – I wonder if Owl survived,' Fox murmured. 'I don't think we'll ever know. Oh, I do yearn to see that poor pompous old bird!'

'Me too,' Badger echoed. 'It just hasn't been the same without him. Even if he is so quarrelsome at times.'

Fox was amused in a sad kind of way. 'I bet Weasel misses their arguments,' he ventured to say.

The sun was well up when they approached Fox and Vixen's earth. They went very warily under the trees. But the foxes were fortunate. Their earth was situated in a copse of immature trees which, with their more flexible trunks and branches, had survived very much better than many of the larger specimens.

'We're lucky,' Fox said to Vixen. 'May you have the same luck, Badger, old friend.'

'We shall see, we shall see,' Badger replied as he trudged on, leaving them behind. He crossed the open space between the foxes' copse and the sloping piece of young beech woodland within which his set had been excavated. He soon noticed that, just as elsewhere in the Park, this patch of woodland was altered beyond recognition. Many well-grown trees had met their deaths during the hurricane's brief but imperious rule. They lay, spanning the ground amongst the litter of branches and brushwood. Badger paused to listen for the tell-tale creaks that might herald the imminent fall of those weakened trees not yet entirely prised from the ground. There was nothing immediately noticeable. He loped his way anxiously around the obstructions in his path. He was not far now from his set. A little farther – and he stopped dead in his tracks. He stared at the crater in the ground which was all that was left of his home, crushed beneath the impact of the fallen tree. Badger was rooted to the spot.

'My – my home,' he whispered. 'I have no home.' Over and over again he muttered the last words. Then, all at once the realization came to him of his narrow escape. He knew that there was no question but that he would have been killed had he stayed where Fox had wanted him to. He recognized the irony of Fox's parting wish. For, despite his new homelessness, Badger *was* lucky. Very lucky indeed. He continued to gaze at the smashed set, wondering how or where he would be able to construct a new home at his advanced age. The thought was not in his mind for long. He had suddenly remembered Mossy.

'Oh! Oh!' he wailed. 'Mole! What's happened to you? Are you buried in there or – or – there at all,' he finished in a whisper.

But Mossy was above ground. After the tree's crash he had surfaced from one of his network of tunnels and he had been timorously waiting and keeping a look-out for Badger ever since. Now he heard his voice and he slowly struggled over the broken and cluttered terrain towards it.

He began to call. 'Badger! Badger! You're safe!'

Badger's head turned at the sound. He saw the little velvet-clad creature pushing through the debris. The two animals rejoiced at the sight of each other.

'Oh Badger, thank goodness you didn't listen to me,' Mossy said fervently. 'Your stubbornness saved you.'

'It did indeed,' Badger replied. 'And your tunnels and home – are they intact?'

'Pretty well,' Mossy said. 'But, poor Badger! Where will you live now?'

'I've no idea,' the old creature admitted. 'I'm a bit long in the tooth to be digging a new home.'

Mossy was silent. He couldn't offer any comfort.

'There's one consolation, though,' Badger went on. 'The Park's ours to roam again. With the threat of Trey removed, I could live – well, just about anywhere. Only, I'd like to be near you, Mole. And *you* live here.'

Mossy was eager to hear about the stag and the rest of the animals. Badger soon told him what he knew.

'Now, what do you think about my idea?' the old creature prompted as soon as the mole was acquainted with events.

'I – I – don't know,' Mossy answered, 'if it would be possible for me to – er – move home now.'

'Oh.' Badger looked crestfallen.

'You see, I have family ties like everyone else – well, *almost* everyone else,' Mossy corrected himself hastily, 'and – and –'

'Of course, I'd forgotten; don't give it another thought,' Badger said at once, kindly. 'I'll manage. Don't worry.'

But Mossy did worry. 'We could stay close anyway, couldn't we?' he offered.

'Well, no, I don't see how we can really,' Badger replied doubtfully. 'You see, the only place I think I can go now is back to that empty set by the Pond. Ah me, I seem to spend all my time going from one end of the Park to the other.'

Mossy was at least cheered by Badger's prospect of ready-made quarters. But he knew they would be distant from each other now and that there was no help for it. The two animals looked at each other sadly.

'Well, well, I'd better be going, Mole,' said Badger. 'I wish I'd stayed where I was, out in the open. I was more than halfway there already.'

'Oh Badger, won't you rest awhile?' Mossy beseeched him. 'You look *so* tired. I'll bring some worms for you. I've plenty to spare. You could at least wait until nightfall before setting off yet again?'

Badger didn't need much persuasion. 'Yes, yes, it would make sense,' he agreed. 'I'll just lie down here for a bit against this tree' – he referred to the one that had smashed his set – 'and have a nap while you rustle up some titbits. And thank you, Mole.'

Fox and Vixen had not been able to put Trey out of their minds. He had made himself their enemy, yet the thought of the stag lying in agony under the crushing weight of a tree niggled at their consciences.

'I suppose he will be found by the Warden,' Vixen conjectured.

'Maybe not for hours – or days,' Fox commented. 'He may be examining quite another section of the Reserve. Look, Vixen,' he said with sudden resolution, 'we can't leave it like this. I feel I want to see for myself what can be done.'

'I'll come with you,' Vixen said, almost with relief.

They headed in the direction they thought most likely to bring them to the wounded stag. They knew he was by the perimeter fence and they guessed it would be at a place not too far from the Pond. In the end they were guided to him without difficulty because they came across the rest of the deer.

Trey had been lying in anguish for a long while. The herd had been unable to help him and he watched the foxes arrive (as he thought) to gloat, with a bitter expression. 'You!' he gasped. 'Couldn't you have . . . left me . . . to my doom?'

'We may be able to help,' Vixen said. 'It's not our way to turn a blind eye to any creature in such terrible distress.'

'What can . . . you do?' Trey panted. 'Puny creatures. . . .'

Vixen ignored his gibe. 'What do you think, Fox?' she asked her partner. 'He'll surely die if that tree isn't moved.'

Fox was racking his brains. He glanced at the other stags who stood about, none of them offering any suggestions. One of them said, 'He's as good as done for. It's only a matter of time.'

'Perhaps not,' Fox said slowly. He was studying the size of the males, their likely strength and the possibility of their using their great antlers. He came to a decision. 'There's only one chance,' he said briskly. 'You males must line up here by the felled tree. Then you must bend your necks and press your antlers against the trunk – all of you, together. You have to try and push it off him.'

The stags muttered amongst themselves.

'Why should we?' asked one bluntly. 'Trey was no friend to us. His day is over.'

'What's *your* interest in helping him?' another one challenged Fox. 'Why do you ask this of us?'

'I'll tell you why,' Fox answered softly. 'Because I picture myself under that tree. It's not difficult to imagine how the poor beast must be suffering.'

His words had a noticeable effect on the male deer. They looked crestfallen; some, a little ashamed. They came forward. Trey watched them in disbelief. He didn't know what to make of Fox, but his pride came to the fore.

'Leave me . . . be,' he whispered. 'I don't ask . . . your help.'

Fox ignored him. The stags hesitated, then continued. Even now some were still in awe of their maimed leader. They set their heads to the bole of the pine and, each straining to his utmost, pushed against the weight of the upended tree. Trey groaned, then bellowed with pain as he felt it shift.

'Harder!' Fox urged. 'It's moving!'

Suddenly the tree half-lifted and then rolled over, leaving Trey free, his gashes and wounds exposed to the onlookers' gaze. He struggled to raise himself but, racked with a terrible agony, fell back again. His crushed and broken limbs could no longer support him. His efforts had exhausted him and he was unable to stir. The other deer backed away, appalled at what they saw.

'We can't leave him like this,' said Vixen.

'Only human intervention can help him now,' Fox replied grimly. 'We must search for the Warden.' He turned a look of compassion on Trey and a flicker of recognition momentarily lit up the stag's glassy eyes.

The foxes moved away. They had not gone far when the human figure they knew so well suddenly confronted them. The Warden had heard Trey's roars of pain and was already on his way to investigate. He recognized the pair of foxes and, for a second, three pairs of eyes met. Then the man went on, leaving Fox and Vixen with a strange feeling of comfort and well-being. They saw he was heading for the wounded beast.

'Do you think there's anything even he can do?' Vixen whispered.

'He has his means,' Fox said. 'Humans have great powers.'

Later, that evening, after his rest, Badger left the

regretful Mossy and stumbled away into the darkness. Mossy wondered when he would see him again and Badger, for his part, had much the same thoughts in his own mind. The old animal didn't hurry himself. A new, lighter wind had sprung up, but a chilly one with the feel of late autumn about it. Badger was wary of any wind now that might dislodge the 'creakers' Fox had warned about, so he kept to the open as far as he could. It was a sensible precaution but one that, unfortunately, made his journey to the substitute home much longer, and this delay was to prove crucial.

18

The Missing Ones

The damage caused by the hurricane throughout the Reserve was extensive. Badger, of course, was not alone in having his home destroyed. And, by the time he had hauled himself to the Pond and crept round its edge to the abandoned set, a whole family of badgers had forestalled him. The set was already tenanted. Badger smelt the smell of his own kind as he snuffled the air. He guessed at once what had happened. At the entrance hole he stopped and listened. Animated badger voices – some young, some older – were all chattering about their luck in finding this new home. Badger sighed. They had beaten him to it, and he had to acknowledge that the extensive tunnels and chambers were more suited to a family than to one ancient, solitary animal. He trudged to the Pond to drink.

Lost in his mournful reflections on the situation, he was unaware that another badger was drinking, only a metre or two away. But she, however, had noticed him and, so familiar a figure was the Farthing Wood badger, she knew at once who he was. She lost no time in trotting to his side.

'It's a pleasure to see you,' she said sincerely.

'Oh!' said Badger with a start. 'Is it?' He looked at the young female.

'What a terrible storm,' said the female. 'I've moved my family here. We lost our old place.'

'Yes. So I gathered. I'm also homeless,' Badger confessed.

'You? Oh no. That's dreadful. But wait – were you –?'

'Yes,' Badger interrupted her. 'I came here on the same quest. But you stole a march on me,' he joked. 'I've no complaints; don't feel bad about it. There's too much space to be wasted on one old male.'

'Oh, but you have to have shelter too,' the female replied feelingly. 'There's plenty of room for one more. Please – we shouldn't care to leave you out in the cold. Do join us. We shan't interfere. You can keep yourself to yourself. And we –'

'No, no, I wouldn't dream of it,' Badger refused. 'You're very kind, I'm sure. I do appreciate it. But I'm not used to sharing. Really, I wouldn't care to start now. I'll be all right. I'll find something.' He had already begun to move off.

'Please,' the female badger called after him. 'Don't go. I'm sure we could work something out quite to your satisfaction.'

'I'm touched by your kindness,' said Badger, but he

didn't turn back. 'Please don't concern yourself about me.' He even increased his pace.

The young female stood looking after him. 'Poor old fellow,' she murmured to herself. 'I do believe he was a little afraid of me.'

'No home now, no home now, not anywhere,' Badger muttered as he wandered about. 'What can I do? I can't live out in the open. Perhaps there's a hole somewhere I can tuck myself into.' That was the best he could hope for. Just a resting-place; a refuge. He didn't expect to find himself a proper set. And, as he wandered and searched and searched and wandered, even the modest demand of a small hole seemed unattainable. The prospect of wandering right through the dark hours without discovering anything seemed a real possibility, as the areas Badger dared to search were limited because of the risks under the trees.

For the first time in his long life Badger came close to despair. He tried reminding himself that, during the animals' long trek from Farthing Wood, he had had to rest and hide in all kinds of unusual places. But he had been younger then, more adaptable and, above all, not alone. Now he was aware of an awful loneliness and he really was too old to cope with this sort of disruption to his life.

'What a way to end up,' he murmured self-pityingly as he sought in vain for a shelter of some kind. He got in such a state that it rather turned his head and he didn't realize where he was going. He wandered through one of the gaps in the broken perimeter fence and out on to the open downland. He didn't know where he was and he went on, blindly searching, as if he were still within the Park. In the end weariness and hopelessness took their toll of the old creature and he simply lay down where he was and went to sleep. Even the cold wind failed to disturb him.

When daylight broke over the grassy expanse Badger woke up, thinking momentarily that he was safe inside his set. His eyes soon told him differently and, with an awful shock, he realized he was no longer even in the Nature Reserve. He felt as if he were in a sort of daze. Nothing seemed quite real any more. He didn't know why he was standing alone on the downland or how he had got there.

'No point going back to that place,' he told himself as he stood looking towards White Deer Park. 'Nowhere for me there.' The rigours of homelessness and solitude had scattered his wits. 'Only one home for old Badger,' he decided as he remembered the comforts of his ancient family set in Farthing Wood. '*That's* where I'll go. Nobody else knows about it. It'll be just for me, like always.' And at that moment he really did believe the set was there waiting for his return.

'Now, let me see, which direction would it be? It's a long way, I know.' He looked about him and settled on his course. Some dim recollection of the way the animals had travelled prompted his decision. 'Hm, yes. I think this is it,' he mumbled as he set off again. 'Toad will know anyway. When I see him he can remind me.'

The cold wind ruffled his bristly coat. Under other circumstances Badger would have known perfectly well that Toad, in such temperatures, would be driven to begin his hibernation. But that sort of reasoning was beyond him now and so, in this sorry state of mind, he went on.

During the next few days the animals speculated about the White Deer herd. The Warden had taken charge of Trey and Whistler had reported that the stag had been removed from the Reserve. 'I doubt if he will be seen again,' he said. 'His injuries were so severe.'

'Only time will tell,' said Fox. 'We did our best for him, at any rate.'

'And if he doesn't return, who will be his successor?' Weasel wondered. 'Let us hope it will be one who recognizes that the Park is for all of us.'

'We can almost depend on that,' said Vixen. 'The blood of the Great White Stag, our friend, is in most of the herd. Trey was not typical. The others are unlike him. They're altogether milder creatures.'

The inhabitants of the Park became used to the presence of men brought in to remove dangerous and fallen trees and to repair the all-important Reserve fencing. The sound of mechanical saws became a regular feature, together with that of hammers and motor vehicles. Naturally the animals kept well away from any human activity but, as time went on and much of the wreckage was cleared away, they were struck constantly by the new look of the Park that was their home. New vistas, new clearings were opened up. The familiar terrain became unfamiliar and for a while the Reserve's inhabitants all felt strange; as if in some way they had been displaced. However, there was one piece of good fortune that resulted from the storm.

On his rounds of inspection the Warden had covered

every corner of White Deer Park. In this way he had discovered the poisonous containers that had been dumped some time ago into the ditch which led into the stream from outside the Park's boundaries. In no time at all these dangerous items had been disposed of, yet it would take a while longer for the water to be rid of its pollution and run clean again. All aquatic life in the stream had been killed. It became the Warden's responsibility to monitor the level of toxicity in the water so that eventually, once the stream was healthy again, re-stocking of fish and other small fry, as well as some vitally necessary vegetation – water-weeds and suchlike – could go ahead.

The ever watchful Whistler kept his friends up to date with events. 'He's testing the water,' he guessed. 'He cleared the rubbish out of it. I think he's trying to make the stream well again.'

Another time the heron notified them, 'The Warden's taking some water away with him. If he's going to drink it, it must be pure.'

'Take care,' Fox warned him. 'Don't risk yourself too soon.'

'There's no danger,' Whistler answered. 'I shan't go close to it until the fish return. Then I'll know the stream runs clear once more.'

But the stream was not the animals' main concern. Their chief worry now was the disappearance of Badger.

No-one knew where Badger had gone. Fox and Vixen had soon found the crushed home of their old friend and had been pointed in the direction of the abandoned set by Mossy. But when they discovered the family of strange badgers in residence, they turned their attentions elsewhere. A meeting was held in the Hollow and everyone was asked to comb each likely spot for a sign of the missing animal. Of course every one of them drew a blank.

Fox feared for the worst. 'I'm afraid we've lost him,' he said to Vixen brokenly. 'He can't be in the Park any more. We've looked everywhere. There's just nowhere else. He's gone outside it, I know he has.'

Mossy was distraught. 'He couldn't find a home, he couldn't find a home,' he kept chanting in his misery.

'*We'll* find him a home all right,' Plucky declared. 'It only needs a few of us to drive out those usurping badgers. We'll save the set by the Pond for *our* Badger.'

'No, no, we certainly shan't,' Fox, his elder, corrected him. 'Your heart's in the right place, Plucky, I know. But the set was never Badger's own. The other animals have just as much right to it. They've settled there and *we* shan't disturb them. Oh, if I could only find the dear old creature I'd dig him a home myself. Yes, if it took all my strength I'd do it.'

'You wouldn't do it alone and you know it,' Vixen told him. 'I have claws too. Do you think I wouldn't want to help?'

'Of course you would,' Fox said. 'But what's happening to us? First Tawny Owl and now Badger. We're losing each other and – and I don't think I can put things right this time. I just can't bear it, Vixen.'

'If Badger's gone outside the Park, then why don't

we go after him?' suggested Weasel. 'He's not so swift-footed that we couldn't soon catch him up.'

'Yes, and which direction would we go in?' Adder demanded. 'Would we all go crawling about over the countryside together? Or take different paths? That way there'd be more than just Owl and Badger numbered among the lost. As it is, if I don't get underground soon I shall be lost anyway. Lost for good if the frost gets to me.'

'Nobody's asking you to hang around,' Weasel pointed out.

'Thank you for your civility,' Adder hissed. 'D'you think I can sleep the winter away without knowing if Badger will be here to greet when I wake again?'

'Well, well, you snakes must become more senti-mental as you get older,' Weasel remarked. 'I've never known you admit to such feelings before.'

'Never you mind about that,' Adder rasped, his demeanour resuming its usual mask of nonchalance. 'I think it was you who was instrumental in driving out Tawny Owl from amongst our company?'

'Never!' Weasel cried. 'Not I! I'd never do such a thing. I acknowledge I may have pulled his leg once or twice but how could I have foreseen the consequences? Why, I've never ceased to rue the day he left. All I want is for us all to be together again especially as – well' – here his voice dropped, even trembling slightly – 'as we all grow older.'

Whistler said, 'I'll fly a reconnoitre now and again. But you know I had no luck seeking out Owl. It may be as unrewarding looking for Badger.'

'There's one advantage,' said Friendly. 'Badger's on the ground. Easier to spot an animal than a bird.'

'I'll do my best,' Whistler promised.

Fox turned to Adder. 'Please don't put yourself at risk,' he advised the snake. 'Toad's already slumbering in his winter quarters. We don't want any more losses.'

'I'll wait awhile,' Adder said firmly. 'There have been no frosts so far. And one thing's for sure. There is no dearth of leaves to bury myself in at night.'

'If you should need extra warmth,' Vixen offered graciously, 'our earth can be the cosiest of places. . . .'

Adder's tongue flickered busily. He was strangely moved. 'D'you know, Vixen,' he said softly, 'that sinking my fangs into that horse's leg, so long ago now, is something I've always considered as one of the best things I've ever done in my life?' The snake's red eyes seemed to glow particularly brightly for an instant and Vixen didn't fail to notice.

'I've never forgotten it,' she whispered, 'and I never shall.'

Whistler began flying over the downland the very same day. His eyes scanned the mass of green for a flash of black and white that would reveal Badger's where-abouts. No other animal had that unmistakable colouring. But while the heron coasted and soared on his broad wings, Badger had paused to rest in the shadow of a large building. He had made uncertain progress but the church under whose walls he now lay sleeping was the first positive reminder to him that he had chosen the correct route. Just like Tawny Owl before him, it was the one recognizable landmark for him in that region. And, even as he snored in the open with his back pressed against the stonework, Tawny Owl and Holly were heading for the very same building from the opposite direction.

19

Home

Tawny Owl's journey back to White Deer Park had not been the happy one he had planned. Holly had taken charge of all hunting activities since he had exhausted himself on the first stage of their flight. She had nurtured him with the plumpest of the prey she had caught, almost as if he were a fledgling. Much as he enjoyed these tasty meals, Owl was only grudgingly grateful as, with each day, he felt he was losing more of his independence. Holly also made sure he didn't overtax his stiffened wing muscles, and of this he was quite glad since as soon as his strength returned fully he intended to end his reliance on her. The only function left to Tawny Owl now, over which Holly could exert no control, was his navigation of their route. One by one the major features of the journey – the river, the area of the Hunt, the motorway, the town – were marked and passed. Now Owl set their course for the church.

Sometimes, when Holly had been particularly irk-
some, he wondered about leaving her in whatever roost
they had chosen that day, and then flying away as she
slept. There were occasions when he definitely wished
to be rid of her. But something always held him back.
He would remind himself that he would lose the very
thing for which he had left White Deer Park in the first
place – a mate. And he was conscious of the fact that he
did owe a debt of gratitude to the female owl. She had
kept him alive when he had been trapped in the beech
at Farthinghurst. So they stayed together and now they
neared the end of their journey.

Holly was constantly asking about when they would
arrive. Tawny Owl always replied that, once the
church was within their sights, they were as good as
home. When at last he spied the building ahead,
feelings of excitement, relief, anticipation and also
uncertainty flooded over him. All along he had dreaded
finding what the storm had done to White Deer Park.
And now that moment had almost arrived. The two
birds flew straight to the church and Tawny Owl,
remembering the indignation of the colony of belfry
bats, led Holly to the nave roof instead where they
perched side by side.

'So this is it at last,' Holly breathed. There was no
mistaking her own excitement. The stars shone brilli-
antly in the wide expanse of sky. It was a perfect night
for hunting. 'I'll waste no time,' she said to Owl. 'The
sooner we eat the sooner we can complete our journey.
And, just think, the next time I hunt it will be in the
Park itself.'

Tawny Owl flexed his supple wings. 'Yes,' he said.

'This is the last occasion when you bring me my food. You must stop treating me like an owlet.'

Holly looked at him askance. She guessed his thoughts. 'There's no need for your friends to know about our arrangement,' she said archly. 'I'm sure they don't watch you hunt?'

'Well no, but –'

'Very well then,' she interrupted. 'I can go on looking after you just as before. You should be grateful to be relieved of the tedium of hunting. You'll have a most comfortable and cosseted old age, I promise you.'

'Look, I don't want. . . .' Owl began peevishly, but it was no good. Holly flew away without listening just as she always did. 'How *am* I to get her to understand?' he fluted in exasperation. He watched the bats darting on their aerobatic flights from the belfry. Then he glanced down and, by the south side of the church he saw an animal stirring in the shadows. The striking striped head of a badger was illuminated by the crisp autumn starlight. Tawny Owl gasped. He could scarcely believe his eyes. In his amazement he almost over-balanced from his perch on the roof. He recognized Badger instantaneously.

'Badger! Badger!' he called and swooped down-wards.

The old animal looked up with a puzzled expression. Then he saw Tawny Owl who alighted next to him.

'What on earth are you doing?' Owl asked in an astounded voice.

'Oh, Owl,' said Badger who was still very confused, 'you shouldn't have come looking for me.'

'I didn't come looking for you,' replied the bird.

'Whatever are you talking about? I haven't seen you at all for the whole of the summer. And wherever are you going?'

'Going?' mumbled Badger. 'Oh – um – going home, Owl. Going home.'

'I should think so. But why have you left it?'

'Left what?'

'Home.'

'Well, we all left it, didn't we, when we travelled across country to the – to the. . . .'

'You're not making any sense,' Tawny Owl interjected. He could tell that something was wrong with Badger. 'Now, tell me again. Where are you going?'

Badger looked at him as if he thought it was the owl who was out of his wits. 'Well – Farthing Wood, of course.'

'FARTHING WOOD?!'

'Yes, I have to get home, you see, because I can't live out in the open. I need shelter and – and –'

'Badger, stop. It seems there's something seriously wrong. Now, what's happened? What's the matter with you?'

'The matter with me?' Badger echoed. 'Well, I should have thought that was obvious. I'm homeless, Owl. That's what I am. Homeless.'

Tawny Owl was able to put two and two together. He realized there had been destruction in the Park and now he dreaded more than ever what he was going to see. But he tried to concentrate on Badger's troubles. 'Your home is White Deer Park,' he prompted. 'Why have you left the others? Where are they?'

'Oh, they're all right,' Badger answered sensibly

enough. 'They didn't lose their homes like me. So they – er – they've stayed put.'

Tawny Owl was moved by his old friend's sad plight. 'Dear Badger,' he said. 'You don't understand. There *is* no Farthing Wood. So you must turn back and go along with me.'

But Badger, who had almost lost his reason, couldn't accept this. 'Of course there's a Farthing Wood,' he disputed. 'What a ridiculous thing to say about the place we all grew up in!'

'Oh Badger, have you no memory?' Owl cried. 'The wood was destroyed! Why ever else would we have left it?'

'It was being destroyed when we left,' Badger agreed, 'but most of it was still there. Well, some of it. . . .' He was beginning to sound uncertain.

'Well, it isn't there now,' Tawny Owl insisted in a loud voice as though Badger might be deaf. 'I've been there – all the way back. There's not one stick left standing. No, not one plant. Everywhere is covered with human dwellings. So you *must* turn back.'

The old animal seemed to be trying to register this information. He couldn't quite grasp it. 'You – you've been there?' he repeated.

'Yes.'

Badger was regaining a semblance of his wits. 'Is that where you've been all this time?'

'A lot of it, yes. I've a long story to tell you.'

'But why did *you* go there?' Badger asked perplexedly as he noticed a second owl skimming towards them.

'Here's one reason,' Tawny Owl replied as Holly

arrived, with her bill crammed with food. 'Now, why don't we all eat together?'

Gradually, with Owl's patient help, Badger's understanding began to return. He saw how his foolishness had resulted from the shock of finding himself without a home. When they were ready, they set off for the Park. Badger was very slow, but Tawny Owl was determined not to let the old creature out of his sight and was quite satisfied to fly in short bursts to accommodate his slower pace. As for Holly, for once she was content to take a back seat.

As they went, Tawny Owl was able to piece together from what Badger told him, how the hurricane had devastated the Park. He learnt of the poisoned stream, too, but that despite everything all his old companions had survived. Then he, in his turn, described to Badger his own adventures and the sad fall of the last relic of Farthing Wood.

'So you see, we only have one home, don't we?' he summed up. 'And that's White Deer Park.'

It was broad daylight as they approached the Nature Reserve. Tawny Owl sought out a suitable entry point for Badger where the fencing was not yet repaired. High in the air, Whistler saw the three travellers, flew closer to make sure his eyes weren't deceiving him and then, with a 'krornk' of utmost delight raced to rouse Fox, Vixen, Weasel and Adder.

So when Badger trudged once more into the Park, the group of friends were there to greet him and the long-lost Tawny Owl.

'I hardly dared hope for this,' Fox murmured

emotionally. 'It's a day like no other. How did you come together?'

'There's much to tell,' Tawny Owl answered joyfully.

'My heart beats for both of you,' Vixen whispered to the two lost ones. 'And, Owl, I see you've not travelled unaccompanied?'

Holly was speechless at the sight of the gathered group, so many of them seemed to her like living legends. Tawny Owl wasn't slow to notice this.

'No, I've had good company,' he said, 'though, as you can see,' he added mischievously, 'it's been difficult for me to get a word in edgeways.'

There was much amusement at his remark, though the animals did not, as yet, understand its irony. Weasel was so relieved to see the return of Tawny Owl that he was quite unable to offer him any banter.

'Well, at long last I can retire,' hissed Adder. 'Sinuous has given me up for lost. I've seen what I wanted to see and I don't wish for any more than that. Badger, Owl – I salute you, though you *have* caused me discomfort. Farewell, All. Till the spring!'

They watched him slither hastily away.

'Come, Badger, old friend,' said Fox. 'We have something to show you.' He led the way and eventually they all arrived at Fox and Vixen's earth. Next to it there were new earthworks. While Badger looked on in wonder, clods of earth were thrown up from within this new construction which landed almost at his feet.

'It's not quite ready yet,' Fox said apologetically. 'But there's a company of busy fox paws digging away, as well as others'. You won't have too long to wait.'

'Me?' Badger murmured. 'Is it for me?'

'Of course it's for you. Who else?' said Fox. 'You're to be our near neighbour. And what could be better than that?'

'Nothing,' said Badger. 'Nothing at all.'

'It'll be your home for ever,' Fox told him. 'We shall stay close together for the rest of our lives.'

Just then Mossy surfaced from the new set. 'The foxes dig so furiously,' he said, 'I'm in danger of being buried.' He rushed to be re-united with Badger.

'I think,' said Tawny Owl to Holly, 'we can safely leave them to it for now. Animals have their own habits and we birds' – here he flapped his wings vigorously – 'we have other occupations. The story of Farthinghurst can wait. As for now, I propose we make a circuit of the Park. I haven't seen it for a while and I need to re-acquaint myself with my best hunting terrain. Come on, I'll show you around.'

Holly promptly followed him as he launched into flight.

'Well!' exclaimed Weasel. 'That's something I *never* thought I'd see.'

Other great reads from **Red Fox**

Further Red Fox titles that you might enjoy reading are listed on the following pages. They are available in bookshops or they can be ordered directly from us.

If you would like to order books, please send this form and the money due to:

ARROW BOOKS, BOOKSERVICE BY POST, PO BOX 29, DOUGLAS, ISLE OF MAN, BRITISH ISLES. Please enclose a cheque or postal order made out to Arrow Books Ltd for the amount due, plus 22p per book for postage and packing, both for orders within the UK and for overseas orders.

NAME _____

ADDRESS _____

_____

Please print clearly.

Whilst every effort is made to keep prices low, it is sometimes necessary to increase cover prices at short notice. If you are ordering books by post, to save delay it is advisable to phone to confirm the correct price. The number to ring is THE SALES DEPARTMENT 071 (if outside London) 973 9700.

Other great reads from **Red Fox**

Discover the great animal stories of Colin Dann

JUST NUFFIN

The Summer holidays loomed ahead with nothing to look forward to except one dreary week in a caravan with only Mum and Dad for company. Roger was sure he'd be bored.

But then Dad finds Nuffin: an abandoned puppy who's more a bundle of skin and bones than a dog. Roger's holiday is transformed and he and Nuffin are inseparable. But Dad is adamant that Nuffin must find a new home. Is there *any* way Roger can persuade him to change his mind?

ISBN 0 09 966900 5   £1.99

KING OF THE VAGABONDS

'You're very young,' Sammy's mother said, 'so heed my advice. Don't go into Quartermile Field.'

His mother and sister are happily domesticated but Sammy, the tabby cat, feels different. They are content with their lot, never wondering what lies beyond their immediate surroundings. But Sammy is burningly curious and his life seems full of mysteries. Who is his father? Where has he gone? And what is the mystery of Quartermile Field?

ISBN 0 09 957190 0   £2.50

Other great reads from **Red Fox**

Enter the gripping world of the REDWALL saga

REDWALL Brian Jacques

It is the start of the summer of the Late Rose. Redwall Abbey, the peaceful home of a community of mice, slumbers in the warmth of a summer afternoon. The mice are preparing for a great jubilee feast.

But not for long. Cluny is coming! The evil one-eyed rat warlord is advancing with his battle-scarred mob. And Cluny wants Redwall . . .

ISBN 0 09 951200 9 £3.50

MOSSFLOWER Brian Jacques

One late autumn evening, Bella of Brockhall snuggled deep in her armchair and told a story . . .

This is the dramatic tale behind the bestselling *Redwall*. It is the gripping account of how Redwall Abbey was founded through the bravery of the legendary mouse Martin and his epic quest for Salmandastron. Once again, the forces of good and evil are at war in a stunning novel that will captivate readers of all ages.

ISBN 0 09 955400 3 £3.50

MATTIMEO Brian Jacques

Slagar the fox is intent on revenge . . .

On bringing death and destruction to the inhabitants of Redwall Abbey, in particular to the fearless warrior mouse Matthias. Gathering his evil band around him, Slagar plots to strike at the heart of the Abbey. His cunning and cowardly plan is to steal the Redwall children—and Mattimeo, Matthias' son, is to be the biggest prize of all.

ISBN 0 09 967540 4 £3.50

Other great reads from Red Fox

THE XANADU MANUSCRIPT
John Rowe Townsend

There is nothing unusual about visitors in Cambridge.

So what is it about three tall strangers which fills John with a mixture of curiosity and unease? Not only are they strikingly handsome but, for apparently educated people, they are oddly surprised and excited by normal, everyday events. And, as John pursues them, their mystery only seems to deepen.

Set against a background of an old university town, this powerfully compelling story is both utterly fantastic and oddly convincing.

'An author from whom much is expected and received.'
Economist

ISBN 0 09 9751801 £2.50

ONLOOKER Roger Davenport

Peter has always enjoyed being in Culver Wood, and dismissed the tales of hauntings, witchcraft and superstitions associated with it. But when he starts having extraordinary visions that are somehow connected with the wood, and which become more real to him than his everyday life, he realizes that something is taking control of his mind in an inexplicable and frightening way.

Through his uneasy relationship with Isobel and her father, a Professor of Archaeology interested in excavating Culver Wood, Peter is led to the discovery of the wood's secret and his own terrifying part in it.

ISBN 0 09 9750708 £2.50

Other great reads from *Red Fox*

THE WINTER VISITOR   Joan Lingard

Strangers didn't come to Nick Murray's home town in winter. And they didn't lodge at his house. But Ed Black had—and Nick Murray didn't like it.

Why had Ed come? The small Scottish seaside resort was bleak, cold and grey at that time of year. The answer, Nick begins to suspect, lies with his mother—was there some past connection between her and Ed?

ISBN 0 09 938590 2   £1.99

STRANGERS IN THE HOUSE   Joan Lingard

Calum resents his mother remarrying. He doesn't want to move to a flat in Edinburgh with a new father and a thirteen-year-old stepsister. Stella, too, dreads the new marriage. Used to living alone with her father she loathes the idea of sharing their small flat.

Stella's and Calum's struggles to adapt to a new life, while trying to cope with the problems of growing up are related with great poignancy in a book which will be enjoyed by all older readers.

ISBN 0 09 955020 2   £1.95